BLOODY MAYHEM DOWN SOUTH II

WAR ZONE

Trayvon D. Jackson

GOOD2GO PUBLISHING

A Bloody Mayhem Down South II
Written by Trayvon D. Jackson
Cover design: Davida Baldwin
Typesetter: Mychea
ISBN: 9781943686414

Copyright ©2016 Good2Go Publishing
Published 2016 by Good2Go Publishing
7311 W. Glass Lane • Laveen, AZ 85339
www.good2gopublishing.com
https://twitter.com/good2gobooks
G2G@good2gopublishing.com
www.facebook.com/good2gopublishing
www.instagram.com/good2gopublishing

I would like to dedicate this book to my father,
Johnny H. Miley. Pops, you'll never be forgotten.

ACKNOWLEDGEMENTS

Once again, thanks to God for making this possible again. I would like to thank the Good2Go team for believing in me. We get stronger together, especially when we're working on the same page. Thanks to my assistant, Latoya M. Moye, for being there for me. I would like to give a shout out to all my fans: thank y'all for rocking and appreciating this slide. The devil tried to slow me down when I was writing this book, and I had a bad toothache. Damn! It was a monster, but I faded it like a soldier. I couldn't let my fans down and abort or prolong the book. I would like to give a shout out to my family and friends from all over Martin County. To anyone that I haven't mentioned, that doesn't mean that I've forgotten about you. With that said, everyone please enjoy *Bloody Mayhem Down South II.*

Solomon's Wisdom . . .

*"A man that hath friends must show himself friendly,
and there is a friend that sticketh closer than a brother."*

~ Proverbs 18:24

PROLOGUE

"Seems like you're ready to go all the way. All the way!" R. Kelly emanated from the speakers of the Malibu Chevy as her seat was reclined backward. He kissed her deeply, sucked on her lips and neck, and then nibbled on her ear.

"Ummm," she moaned out when he slid his hand underneath her H&M skirt and caressed her wet pussy and throbbing clitoris.

"You so wet, baby gal," the paymaster said to Trina as he descended and spread her legs apart as he passionately began eating her pussy.

"Ummm, yes! Eat this!"

Boom! Boom! Boom! Boom!

* * *

"I don't like this one, Holmes," Det. Mark Harris said to his partner, who he had pulled from her bed—and vacation—as she ducked under the yellow caution tape.

"Who is she?" Holmes asked, staring at a bullet-riddled Trina and her trick.

"Trina Fox. She's the tip-off that helped the FBI out a couple months ago, and him," Harris said, pointing at the trick, "a full-blown AIDS trick."

"Looks like death two ways. So, she's definitely the target, huh?"

"What other way could we put it? She's logged in as a CI," Harris explained.

"So, the killer follows them to Sandsprit Park, walks up on them while they're getting their groove on, and hands them a whole clip."

"A clip of straight hollow points," Harris corrected.

"And who do we put behind this one?" Holmes inquired.

"I'm looking at the Swamp Mafia. I don't know 'bout you, but I see Jermaine Wilkins's name all over this one."

"It's too easy. He'll never give us something so simple. Maybe it's made to look like him," Holmes assumed.

"There's only one way to find out."

"I doubt he'll talk without a lawyer, Mark," Holmes said, adding, "What trick do you have up your sleeves?" She knew her partner's flexible techniques for getting accurate information from the streets.

"Just let me work my magic," Harris retorted.

ONE

The streets in Hobe Sound/Banner Lake were crowded with folks from every hood in Martin. It was a block party thrown for Capo's eldest brother, Juvie, who jumped yesterday from doing a six-year bid in prison.

Like his brother Capo, Juvie was a yellow-skin nigga who grew up in the lethal streets of Palm Beach County. But he had migrated after the death of his father.

Juvie stood five eight and weighed 155 pounds, and he was always ready to put a nigga in the dirt. He was fresh in his all-black fitted jeans, timbos, and a wifebeater. Around his neck, he sported a thick Cuban link with a phat-ass Jesus charm.

"Juvie, welcome home!" a hot-ass little girl in her teens named Jada shouted to the hot commodity.

When Juvie blew her a kiss and winked at her, she blushed and then walked off with her crowd.

"Girl, you need to stop being so fast!" Jada's sister, Dree, said to her loud enough for Juvie to hear.

When Juvie and Capo looked down the road, they saw a parade of tricked-out box Chevy Caprices, Impalas, and Crown Vics lined up coming down Date Street, beating the block with their thunderous systems.

"Who the fuck is these niggas?" Juvie asked Capo.

"Oh, they my niggas! That's Swamp Mafia," Capo said to Juvie, whose mind went instantly on jack boy mode. The grapevine spoke fondly of Swamp Mafia.

The first Chevy, a cream 1987 Caprice Landau coupe halted in front of Capo, who was holding a bottle of Seagram's gin in his hand. The passenger window came down.

"What's up, dirty?" T-Gutta said to him.

"Just holding it down with my big brah. He finally home. Hey, Juvie, check it out!" Capo called out to his brother, who stood in the background.

Juvie walked up to where Capo stood and checked out the twenty-eight-inch rims on T-Gutta's two-door Chevy.

"Meet the nigga who helped me rise to today, brah. T-Gutta, this is Juvie, my older brother."

"I think I remember him from when y'all use to come stay at y'all's grandma's house on the back street," T-Gutta said.

"Yeah, what they do?" Juvie retorted, bumping fists with T-Gutta.

"You tell me you see money. Is you ready to get down or what?" T-Gutta asked.

"I'm 4-Life. All day, brah."

"And we Swamp Mafia that fuck with the 4-Life heavy," T-Gutta informed Juvie.

"Then I'm always down for the cause, brah. 4-Life!" Juvie stated, throwing up four fingers on his right hand.

"Every move we make is the cause, brah. Welcome home. Tonight when I do business with ya, lil brother, I'ma have something in there for you," T-Gutta promised. "And, Juvie . . ."

"Yeah,"

"It's on the house. You don't owe me nothin'. Just be careful. If you get to sit on it, sit on it, dirty," T-Gutta said as he put flame to a kush blunt. "Get to know the faces of your dollars. Every Benjamin ain't Benjamin. The moment you pick the wrong face, it could be a trap. It's too much money out here to get entrapped, feel me?"

"All day. I smell ya, brah!" Juvie said to T-Gutta.

"Well, Capo, I gotta hit it. Y'all niggas be on key and on point tonight," T-Gutta said.

"Always, brah. Money on time," Capo said as he gave T-Gutta dap.

Juvie watched T-Gutta pull off, and all he could think of was coming up off his dick to be on his level.

I can't get out here movin' fast. I got to take it slow, Juvie thought.

"Brah, look how that bitch Krystal eatin' you up," Capo informed Juvie about the red bitch across the street.

When Juvie looked her way, she quickly turned her head.

"Who she fuckin' with, lil brah?" Juvie asked as he took a swig from his bottle of Remy Martin.

"As of now, nobody, which means you're fresh meat, and she all over you, brah."

Before Capo could do any more encouraging, Juvie walked off and made his bold introduction to Krystal.

"Damn, nigga! What took you so long?" Krystal said.

"I thought you were cross-eyed and lookin' at another nigga," Juvie retorted, getting a chuckle out of Krystal.

"So what made you Pee-Wee Herman tap dance over here?"

"You call that tap dancing?" Juvie inquired.

"What you call it?"

"I call it, put our fronts to the side for one day. I been gone fo' six years. You know what it was before I left and used to come down here. So let's stop playin' games," Juvie said to Krystal, who was burning in ecstasy every moment she stood in his presence.

Something inside made her want to run like a little girl, but they weren't young anymore. She had turned into a gorgeous pecan five foot five, 130-pound twenty-four-year-old who was in college working hard on her master's. And although Juvie had grown just an inch, he was a man.

"I feel that, Juvie, but I'm not one of them easy-to-get hos. I'd rather you go hang out and we just be friends. All that hitting me in one night ain't gonna cut it with me," Krystal explained.

"I can respect that, beautiful. Just don't take your word back, feel me?" Juvie asked.

"Yeah, I feel you," Krystal spoke, praying that she didn't blow her chances with Juvie by turning him down.

* * *

"Damn, brah. I hate that you goin' in at this stage of the game. You gonna miss the club opening," Real said to Shamoney, who was due to turn himself over to the authorities to serve his forty-eight-month sentence.

It was the least amount of time his lawyer could get the state down to from the original sentence of ten years. So, he was grateful for the time. He just hated leaving his wife and kids behind. Chantele had brought him two twin girls who were beautiful just like her.

Allowing Gina to stay in one of the guest rooms was a hard nail to pull off at first; however, Chantele saw that she was no threat. She also felt bad for her, since she had lost her hearing and the doctors couldn't find out why. Her story about seeing Black made her sound insane, and no one believed her.

4

"Yeah, I hate it too, brah, but I gotta do what I gotta do. The sooner, the better. I just want to make it back home to see my kids grow," Shamoney said to his brother.

They were lounging out back by Shamoney's pool, enjoying the delicious food cooked by Chantele that consisted of curried goat, chicken, yellow rice, cabbage, and sweet cornbread. It was Shamoney's last meal, cooked from the soul.

"Don't worry, lil brah. I'ma be here every day and every step of the way for you and with you, brah. You not gonna miss nothing, because you gonna be there also," Real told his brother.

"There you niggas go!" Johnny said as he walked out the back sliding door with Su'Rabbit.

They were both holding bottles of vodka in their hands.

"What's up, Chyna Man?" Shamoney spoke.

"I couldn't miss my second eldest brother's going-away party. Shit 'bout to turn up."

"Chyna Man, this ain't no party," Shamoney corrected.

"Shit! I know that. Ain't no babies out in the pool or Boosie playing from the speakers. Of course, this ain't no party!" Johnny said.

"What's up, Su'Rabbit?" Shamoney asked.

"Listen, I'm sure ya brother Real done gave you the game already. Don't drop the soap," Su' said, getting a chuckling going.

"Fuck you two clowns!"

"Swamp Mafia, baby!" Real exclaimed.

"Damn! I'ma miss y'all niggas," Shamoney said.

"Don't worry. We gonna hold you down, brah!" Johnny said, giving his brother Shamoney a hug.

Shamoney wasn't due to turn himself over to the authorities until sunrise. As the night neared, everyone came and wished him well. At 10:00 p.m., Chantele came downstairs and stole Shamoney away from his friends, and the party subsequently dissipated, and everyone went about their way.

Chantele and Shamoney made love like never before until the sun came up, and it was time for him to depart. The hardest part was leaving his kids and a burdensome Gina behind. Shamoney had paid for an instructor to teach Gina body and sign language, as well as a personal psychologist to help her overcome her increasing dementia-like state.

Neither Shamoney nor anyone else was buying her story that Black had placed voodoo on her, which caused her to go deaf. Yet the doctors still could not discover what made her suddenly lose her hearing.

Gina's three girls were in good hands with Pat's mother, who lived in Miami. Pat's mother had full custody and was battling to keep them, against Gina's protests. Before Pat retaliated on her for cheating, he had filed for divorce and claimed that during her infidelity, she would have sex in front of the kids. A dead man's allegations seemed to hold more weight against a deaf woman's word. Gina was miserable, and each day it seemed as if she only got worse.

TWO

Since Real had taken over, 5th Street in the swamp had become a main strip like New York and LA, where no one slept. The fiends were coming from all over to buy the good crack. V-Money had his lil soldiers trapping on every block in the swamp. He was getting rid of fifty kilos in a week and extending his reach all the way to Okeechobee and Palm Beach. V-Money quickly became Real's top hustler and had control of the streets. V-Money was wise, and he knew when and when not to hustle.

Jake's store was still the spot where hustlers came to get off their product. Real had bought Jake's property and was also soon opening one of the biggest clubs on the Treasure Coast. The club was being built in Port St. Lucie off of I-95 and Gatlin Boulevard. Everyone was eager to see it open. Since Real was always on the go, he let V-Money manage the store. V-Money and Lunatic were inside playing PS3 NFL Madden when Lala entered with her daughter, Destiny.

"Money, I hope that y'all don't have no stale-ass chips in here," Lala said.

"You come in here every week with yo' criticism. How 'bout you take that up with the—"

Boc! Boc! Boc!

"Oh shit!" V-Money exclaimed, immersing behind the counter and coming back out with his MAC-10.

The shots were outside. Lunatic followed suit as V-Money ran to the front door after leaping over Lala, who had hit the ground with Destiny at the first shot.

Boc! Boc! Boc!

The shots came through the door and missed V-Money by an inch.

Shit! he thought as he kicked open the door and ran outside after the fleeing SUV.

He let his MAC-10 rapidly spit, to no avail of hitting any target. When the SUV turned right on Charleston, it was gone. V-Money looked around saw two of his workers slumped over and lying next to their weapons.

"Shit!" V-Money exclaimed as he looked at the two teens, who were high school freshmen dropouts.

A crowd quickly gathered around the two teens. It was evident from their brains pouring out of their heads that there was no reason to rush and call 911. The killers were long gone, and the victims were no doubt dead.

* * *

The murder rate was crazy. It was transparent to Real that Pat's death was just another man down. Black still had niggas in the Haitian mafia standing up for him. He knew about Big Chub, who had inevitably taken over Pat's position. All Big Chub had to say was "go," and murder was the only outcome. Kids were killing kids and making themselves each other's rivals. When V-Money hit Real with the news of the drive-by shooting, all he could do was say, "Damn!"

It was sad to see teens taking out their own generation. This was never part of Real's plans to take over, but he understood the method. Every action is a reaction, just like every positive needs a negative.

Real rose from bed and prepared himself to go meet up with his connect. When his feet hit the plush carpet, Bellda awoke from her sleep, and she wrapped up in the excess covers.

"When will you be back, baby?" she spoke up, with sleep in her voice.

"I'll be in by twelve o'clock, if you still up."

"Well, I guess I'll make us some dinner."

"I love it," Real retorted.

"You have no choice," Bellda said as Real finished putting on his clothes.

"Oh yeah!" Real said as he came back to the bed and kissed Bellda on the lips. "I swear the taste of you could never get old," Real complimented.

"I was thinking the same thing 'bout you," Bellda said, rubbing on Real's nicely toned chest.

"I love you, beautiful," Real said as he kissed Bellda again.

"I love you too, daddy," she said seductively.

When Real stepped outside in the sunset, he could instantly sense the bloodshed in his city. He hopped inside his smoke-gray .745 and turned up Boosie's "Long Clips and Choppas." Real serenaded Boosie's lyrics as he gingerly maneuvered through traffic. He badly wanted to spark up a blunt, but he knew the rules prohibited him from doing so when he was driving one of his stash cars. In fact, Real made up the rules himself.

When Real pulled up to T-Gutta's crib, he honked the horn twice. He was still laying his head in the hood on Tarpon despite having the money to move into a mansion.

"He's coming, Real," LeLe stuck her head out the door and shouted.

While Real waited, he saw a young nigga in his teens making a drug sale.

Lil niggas out here really getting it, I see, Real thought.

But his thoughts were interrupted when T-Gutta came around and hopped into the passenger's seat.

"You ready for this?" Real asked T-Gutta, who seemed to be nervous.

"Hell yeah. I've been ready since we first clicked," T-Gutta said as Real pulled off.

Today was Real's last day of meeting with his connect to do transactions and traffic. T-Gutta and Lunatic would be over picking up the drop and getting it to V-Money to distribute. Real would be too busy chasing down Big Chub and Black to deal with everything else—without Shamoney. About forty-five minutes later, Real pulled up to a Holiday Inn in Palm Beach County and parked beside a black Suburban.

"Lunatic will stay in the car while you hop into the backseat with everything. This button here is to access the safe box," Real explained while showing T-Gutta a red button under his seat.

"Grab the bags. Let's go! Remember, Lunatic stays in the car, and he's supposed to be watching everything that moves," Real informed T-Gutta as he grabbed the two duffel bags from the hidden safe box in the backseat.

"Let's handle business," Real said as he tossed the bag of money to T-Gutta.

Real attentively watched as T-Gutta and Chucky conducted business in the backseat of the Suburban. He then hit up Pablo to let him know that business had been taken care of. His next step would be to visit Polo in Ft. Lauderdale to see Polo, to whom he had taken a serious liking.

* * *

"Bitch, you lied to me and cheated on me! For what?"

"Please don't kill me. I love you!" she screamed to her possessed husband as he came closer to her, backing her into a table.

She kept her eyes on the gun in his hand. She stumbled backward on the glass table and shattered it into tiny diamonds.

"Please don't! Please! I love you!" she cried out, but her cries weren't being honored.

He had no soul and no mercy for her. Without anywhere else to run, he stood over her, aimed at her face, and then pulled the trigger.

Boom!

"No! No! No!" Gina screamed as she came out of her sleep all sweaty and afraid.

The home nurse quickly came to Gina's aid with a cold towel to wipe away her sweaty face and chest.

"No! No!" Gina continued.

"It's okay, baby. You're okay!" the black nurse said, knowing that Gina couldn't hear her.

Nurse Addie was an old woman in her mid-sixties, who had been caring for mentally ill patients for more than thirty years. She quickly calmed down Gina, who began sounding like a chicken, something she had grown accustomed to doing throughout the day.

"I hate when you get like this on me. Only God knows what's really wrong with you," the nurse exclaimed while filling a syringe with sedation medication to put Gina back down into a coma-like state. "Now just a moment, child. Let me find a vein." When she found Gina's good vein, she injected the hound dog medicine and rocked her back to sleep with less trouble. "God, heal this woman. Please bring her back to this world. For you know she didn't come into this world this way," Nurse Addie prayed to her Christian God.

Chantele walked into the room a second later and saw Addie tucking in Gina. "Is she okay?"

"Yeah, she'll be okay, baby," Addie retorted.

"I feel sorry for her," Chantele spoke.

"Don't we all, honey. I just don't understand, but it's not my ultimate place to try to find out. Only God knows her reasons," Addie explained.

"Yeah, I can agree," Chantele responded.

THREE

When T-Gutta pulled up to the crowd of niggas standing on Date Street in Hobe Sound, Capo, Trap Money, and Juvie all dispersed from the crowd and walked over to his car. It was evident that they were shooting craps, from the money in their hands.

"What's good, 4-Life?" T-Gutta asked them all.

"Throwing fours, fucking hos, and getting this money," Capo replied.

"Three hos, one me, Gutta!" Trap Money said.

"What's good, Juvie? Are you enjoying this shit?" T-Gutta asked.

"Man, this shit's beautiful, brah. I appreciate you lookin' out."

"It's no problem. Just stay out, my nigga, and get this money with us, feel me?" T-Gutta replied to Juvie.

"Fo' sure," Juvie said.

"Check it out, though, at 12:00 a.m. I'ma spin through. Y'all be at the spot. I got some work fo' y'all!" T-Gutta exclaimed. "Real wants y'all to handle something in your backyard over on 6th."

"We got you, my nigga," Juvie stated.

In downtown Palm Beach, T-Gutta had a few cats to deal with who were refusing to pay for the spotted kilos he had fronted them weeks ago. Word had gotten back from one of them, who was still fucking with T-Gutta, that they had a new connect. T-Gutta wanted to step down on the niggas that called themselves D-Boyz, but he had some other ruthless niggas who would not stick out like a sore thumb.

When T-Gutta left Capo, Trap Money, and Juvie, he bumped into a bad bitch named Shada, who he had been fucking on and off. He scooped her up and then retired for the afternoon with her to a hotel room in Hobe Sound.

* * *

Lala and her clique of Ms. Gorgeouses were making a killing today. The credit card scam had elevated to tax fraud, and they were completely looking like new money. They were in Tampa visiting their home girls Katina and Dawn, who had taught them the tax game. It was easy and addictive. In just three weeks, the clique had racked up half a million in tax fraud.

"Girl, I swear y'all better slow y'all asses down, hitting Mr. Sam is only a seasonal thing, Lala," Katina warned.

"I know, sis. I'ma slow down and tell the girls the same," Lala retorted.

Katina was gorgeous. She stood five foot three and weighed 145 pounds, and she was shaped like a Coke bottle. Her twin, Dawn, lived in Atlanta with her fiancé, Trayvon.

Lala and Katina were in the kitchen preparing dinner for the rest of the girls, who were on their way from shopping.

"I keep telling you, Lala, that you need to move up here. Tampa is beautiful. Every time I see the news update on my phone, it's always Martin County, St. Lucie County, Palm Beach County, and last night it was Okeechobee County. And it's always murder, murder, murder!" Katina exclaimed. "I'm worried about you and Destiny. You have the money to move into a beautiful home, sis."

Truth was Lala didn't want to leave Real, despite having a loving and caring man in her life, yet Birdman was not her dream.

"I'll think about it, but I first have to talk to the girls, Katina. I promise, okay?" Lala stated as she hugged her friend, who seemed distressed about Katina's safety.

"I have four kids and lost my baby boy to a stray bullet. He was only six years old and playing in the living room when a bullet came through the window and struck him. Save Destiny while you can, Lala," Katina explained.

Lala was aware of Katina having lost a child, but she never knew that the cause was a stray bullet.

"God is speaking to you," Katina said as she walked out of the kitchen to set the table in the dining room.

"I know he is," Lala whispered to herself.

I got to move on and let Real go before I lose more than I'd ever expect, she thought.

* * *

When Juvie pulled up to the Arab corner store on 6th Street in downtown Palm Beach, he saw a fiend he had known all his life, named Brahman.

"You reckon Braham knows where D-Bo at?" Juvie inquired of Capo and Trap Money.

"Hell yeah!" Trap Money replied from the backseat of the stolen auto.

"Yo, Brahman. Check it out!" Juvie called out, after dropping down his window.

"What's up, young'in?" Braham questioned.

Juvie stuck his hand out the window and dropped five 20-piece-sized rocks of cocaine into Brahman's hand.

"This ain't Christmas. Tell me where to find D-Bo?" Juvie asked.

"Oh! Oh! Oh! He stay on 8th in the apartment complex. Pinewood Place. Room, room 305. He's there right now, nephew," Brahman stuttered.

Click! Clack!

"You sure?" Juvie asked, cocking back the slide on his Glock .40.

"Positive, nephew," Brahman said.

Juvie knew that if he gave a fiend more than expected, he would get any information he wanted. And that's why he had to do what he had to do.

"Bet that up, Brahman."

Boom! Boom! Boom

Juvie refused to leave Braham alive. He would give up Juvie for less than what it cost him to give up D-Bo.

"You fiends can never be trusted!" Juvie exclaimed as he pulled off, leaving Brahman dead as a doornail with three slugs to his face.

"How did I know you were going to do that?" Capo asked his brother.

"Because you know how 4-Life lives, of course."

* * *

When Juvie pulled up to the Pinewood Place, he saw that the place was deserted and peaceful. Though looks could be deceiving, Juvie knew that Pinewood Place was yet another jungle into which he was stepping. He pulled around back and kept a close visual on room 305. The lights were on, and two niggas had stepped out the moment Juvie killed the headlights.

"Trap Money, when we step out, take the wheel and keep it hot," Juvie informed his friend to keep the engine running.

"I got ya, brah."

"Let's go, Capo," Juvie said as he pulled his skully down over his head.

Juvie and Capo stepped out of the car and made a dash toward the apartment. There were two niggas outside with their backs to Juvie and Capo as they crept up on them.

"What's up, D-Boyz?" Juvie said, startling them.

"Oh shit!" one exclaimed, trying to flee and pull out his pistol.

However, Capo nailed him with his Glock 19.

"Back into the apartment, nigga," Juvie demanded the other one, who played it calm.

When the door opened, Juvie caught D-Bo lying back on the couch getting his dick sucked. Apparently he didn't hear the shots outside the apartment, as evidenced from the loud music playing from the surround system. When D-Bo saw his homie Terral walk into the living room, he mistook him as wanting to join the party, until he heard the shot that exploded Terral's head.

"Oh shit!" D-Bo was startled. He jumped up and tried reaching for his AK-47 but was chopped down by Juvie's Glock, which hit him high in his gut and groin. "Ahh!" D-Bo cried out.

"Bitch, what you looking at?" Capo said to the girl before he shot her twice between the eyes.

Both Juvie and Capo stood over D-Bo and emptied their clips into him. Together they slammed in another full clip and then made a dash from the apartment. Trap Money met them halfway. The trio left the scene and then hopped on I-95 northbound back to Martin County, where Capo called T-Gutta with the job well done.

* * *

Since giving up Pat as a sacrifice to the gods, Black had made his nephew Big Chub his new second-in-command. Big Chub was a more calculated, strategic warrior when it came to fighting off the enemy. Black was back in Miami Gardens, where the killing had done dramatic numbers due to the beef between the Haitian Mafia and the Zo'pounds.

Together, Black and Big Chub pulled up to an old warehouse on 179th. The Haitian chauffeur and bodyguard opened the back door of the limousine. Seeing that it was clear, he gave Black the okay to step out. Black and Big Chub then walked into the warehouse and saw that the person they had come to meet was waiting for them.

"Well, I wouldn't have believed it without my own eyes, Stanley," Black said to bound FBI agent Mike Stanley.

Two of Black's bodyguards were standing on each side of Stanley, who had been badly beaten with a spiked chain.

As Stanley stared at Black, he began to shit himself all over again.

"So tell me, how does it feel for the prey to capture the hunter?" Black asked.

"Davis will kill you, Black." Stanley yelled in pain from his broken ribs.

"Are you sure you want to remind me 'bout my so-called predestined fate?" Black asked.

"Do us all a favor and turn yourself over, Black. My people know exactly where I am." Stanley winced in pain again. "They will kill everything in here."

Black wasn't moved by the false threat. He knew that Agent Stanley was lying straight through his bloody grill. Stanley had been on vacation in South Beach when he and his wife were abducted by Black's men. Stanley had watched his wife get raped and then slaughtered like a wild animal.

"Agent Stanley, I would love to face Davis, but unfortunately it's impossible for him to find either of us at the moment. For ten years, you two desperately have been trying to bring me down, but the gods wouldn't allow me to fall. I know your every move, Stanley," Black said as he pulled out a buck knife from the waist of his black jeans. "Like I knew that you guys would join my sacrifice party back at the hotel where you killed Pat," Black continued as he grabbed a handful of Stanley's salt-and-pepper hair and yanked his head back while staring into his eyes.

Lord, please save me from this monster! Stanley prayed introspectively.

"Tell me everything I need to know. Why is it that you muthafuckas can't stop looking for me?" Blacked inquired.

God, save my soul! Stanley thought before he spoke.

"Black, fuck you and your life. You will surely die and burn in hell!"

Before Stanley could finish his insults, Black quickly slit his throat from ear to ear. Agent Stanley was dead instantly.

"Crucify him and give him to the gods before dawn comes," Black ordered his men, who immediately began preparing Stanley to be nailed to a cross.

"Nephew, let's go. We have important matters to attend to," Black said to Big Chub as they turned on their heels.

When Agent Tod Davis received the disturbing news that halted his three-week vacation in Cancun, he was flown out by private jet to Miami, where he found the crime scene of his life.

"I can't believe this shit!" Davis cried out to his boss, director of the FBI Tom Johnson, who was an ex-CIA in his mid-fifties. He stood tall at six three and weighed 225 pounds. He was a black man who seriously wanted to drink the blood of Jean Black Pierre.

"We have to put this dog down, Davis, and I mean as soon as possible," Johnson stated.

Both agents and crime scene investigators were staring at the gruesome sight of their fellow agent who was nailed to a cross like Jesus.

"Do we have any witnesses?" Davis asked his boss, who shook his head negatively.

"No one saw anything, but the Haitian mafia is taking full ownership," Johnson said, pointing at the graffiti on the cross.

Agent Davis took a closer look and almost fainted when he saw his loved one's names followed by the name of his deceased wife.

"Apparently, Mr. Black has stopped running and hiding and has decided to hunt the prey instead," Johnson explained.

"Do you need to be relieved from this case, Davis?"

"Boss, Jean Black Pierre don't scare me."

Before Davis could get his next words out, he vomited everywhere.

"He crossed me! That's it. I'ma bring him down, boss. Please don't take me off the case," Davis begged, hunched over with his hands on his knees.

"We'll give it a try. If it becomes too much, I'm taking you off the case, deal?" Johnson said.

"Deal, boss," Davis answered.

FOUR

Like everyone else in the world, Real was watching the Miami news and the face of his enemy being broadcast. Bellda was in shock when she heard that the head of the Haitian mafia had struck again within ten years.

"Baby, this man got to be crazy!" Bellda exclaimed while looking at the face of Black on the news.

"Yeah, that shit he did is gonna have him famous forever," Real admitted.

"It's voodoo that he supposedly left behind. Calling it a damn sacrifice."

Real grabbed the remote control from the nightstand and shut off the television.

"What do you think about this voodoo shit?" Real questioned.

He was worried, because he didn't really want to expose his fear of his enemy possibly casting a spell on him.

"My mama always told me that in order to be affected by the works of voodoo, you'd have to believe in it first," Bellda said to Real as she climbed on top of him and straddled him.

"So, if I don't believe in it, don't worry about it?"

"Exactly, baby," Bellda retorted as she kissed Real on the lips.

"Do you believe in it?" he asked her.

"No, baby. I never even been to Haiti to even be 'round those who do," Bellda answered.

Real instantly began thinking about Gina and what she had declared before she lost her mind. She had told the doctors,

Real , and Shamoney that she saw Black come into the room while they were visiting her.

"Gina's deaf, and no one has any idea what caused it, not even the doctors," Real explained to Bellda.

"So that's why she sounds like a chicken now?" Bellda asked, not meaning to sound sarcastic.

"Something happened to her that no one can explain," Real said.

"Well, let's not worry about it right now. I need some dick," Bellda said as she slid down in bed, pulled out Real's dick through the slot in his briefs, and then slowly began to suck his cock.

"Deal!" he exhaled.

* * *

Killa County
Fort Pierce City

"Chyna Man, let me holla at you for a moment," one of Johnny's workers, Demon, said.

"What's good, homie?" Johnny asked while sitting on the trunk of his Chevy Impala SS.

"Man, shit over on 7th Street spooking me out, brah!"

"What do you mean by that, Demon?"

"Shit! Money too good, and I don't have the supply I need. So I'm wondering if we can get more product so we won't be losing money waiting on re-up," Demon suggested.

Johnny thought for a moment. What Demon was really telling him was that it was time to step up on the quantity of supplies. And the only person who could do that was his brother Real. "I'ma see what I can do and get back to you."

"Bet that up, my nigga," Demon retorted as he gave Johnny dap before he strutted off.

"Yo, Chyna Man!" a fiend called out while walking up from behind the projects building with his fist balled tightly holding money.

"What's good?" Johnny asked the filthy fiend.

"Man, I need a twenty, and I mean a phat twenty piece."

"Well, do you have phat twenty piece money?" Johnny asked.

"Yeah, hear me out first. I only got—"

Before the fiend could finish, Johnny pulled out his .44 Bulldog and aimed it at the fiend's head.

"What the fuck I tell you 'bout coming to me short of money? You think I'm out here risking my freedom and life 'cause you want to come short of my money?" Johnny screamed at the startled fiend.

"Naw, nephew, it ain't even like that. See, what I was trying to tell you was that I got eighteen dollars."

Boom! Boom! Boom!

Johnny wasn't trying to hear that shit. He popped the fiend three times in the head. When he looked around, he only saw two witnesses, but they both walked back into their apartments. Johnny then got in his car and reversed over the dead fiend, leaving a more gruesome sight, as the confines of the fiend's stomach poured out of his mouth.

"Muthafucka come to me half-stepping. It's too much money out here to come to me short of money," Johnny said as he called up one of his bitches who lived on Airport Road in the area.

Her name was Dominique, and she was one of his favorites.

"Hello," Dominique answered.

"Daddy's on his way home. You know how I want it."

"Boy, you a mess. You better hurry up, because I have to go to work soon," she retorted.

"Say no more," Johnny replied.

When Johnny pulled up to Dominique's crib, he parked his Impala backward. Dominique was a married woman whose husband stayed on the go working as a movie director. Johnny had last heard that he was in New York. Still, Johnny wasn't going to take any chances. It was routine, and he wasn't changing up for anything in the world. As he walked toward the front door, Dominique opened it wearing only a towel from hopping out of the shower.

"Baby all wet for me, huh?" Johnny said as he pulled her into his arms and gripped her succulent ass all at once.

Johnny closed the front door with his foot and then pinned Dominique against the door. He then locked the door to secure his safety. He kissed her deeply while she unfastened his jeans and then pulled out his erect dick. She stroked him to his capacity while drowning in his deep-throat kisses. Dominique was a sexy five foot four, 125-pound dark-skinned bitch who had a striking, scintillating, voluptuous body.

"Mmm!" she moaned out when Johnny began to suck on her neck.

He stepped out of his jeans, picked her up, and carried her over to the comfortable plush sofa. When he laid her down, Johnny began planting small kisses down her body from her lips to her breasts.

"Baby, please!" Dominique panted as he continued to sexually torture her.

When Johnny made it to her sultry mound and stuck his fingers inside her wetness, her body began to tremble.

"Uhh shit, daddy!" she purred.

Johnny sucked, licked, and ate her pussy until she came like crazy. She was a squirter, and Johnny loved it every time he made her squirt. Dominique was panting and begged him to fuck her.

"Baby, please fuck me!"

Johnny stood up and began stroking himself. "Put that ass in the air for daddy," he demanded.

Dominique wasted no time following orders. When she got on all fours with her ass airborne, Johnny deeply plunged inside her world.

"Uhh shit!" she cried out in ecstasy.

* * *

"That's a swamp nigga," Crazy Zoe said to his twin brother, Boxhead.

They were Haitian mafia Zoes and had just left the Treasure Coast Mall shopping for some new shoes and clothes. Crazy Zoe was the eldest of the two. They were both very swarthy, with foreign features and a heavy Haitian accent when they spoke English.

"I know they swamp niggas because I did time with the tall one. That's Kenny," Crazy Zoe explained.

"What? You want to hit 'em up or just give it to them?" Boxhead asked.

"Chub said to flip these niggas on every corner. Then that's what we gonna do," Crazy Zoe said as he started the engine.

"Let's follow them until we get somewhere to hit 'em up good," Boxhead recommended.

"Yeah, we'll trail 'em," Crazy Zoe retorted as they began trailing the black-on-black Charger.

* * *

Shamoney wasn't a happy camper being hundreds of miles away from home. He was hoping to end up in a nearby prison closer to home. Despite him being housed in the Florida panhandle at Century Correctional, Chantele still got on the road with her twins and Shada Jr. to visit Shamoney. He was happy to see his family when he stepped into the visitor lobby in his fresh blue prison state uniform.

"Hey, baby," Chantele spoke as she stood up, hugged, and then kissed her man.

"Damn, woman! I miss you like crazy. Talkin' on the phone will never compensate the value of actually seeing your beautiful face, baby." He then looked at the kids. "And how are my babies doing?" Shamoney asked as he reached in and grabbed his two daughters and brought Shada Jr. into a warming embrace as well. He kissed them all, no more, no less. "Boy, you getting big!" Shamoney acknowledged.

Shada Jr. was happy to see his father. He clung to his leg like it was the last thing in the world to hold on to.

"You miss me, boy?" Shamoney asked Shada Jr. as he picked him up and sat him on his lap.

"All he says is 'Daddy' to me, and he won't even say it to nobody else. What do you want to eat? I'll go grab it while I give you time with the kids," Chantele said.

"Anything will be fine. Whatever you eat, I'll eat, baby."

"Okay," Chantele retorted as she strutted off to stand in the food line.

While Chantele stood in line, Shamoney admired her beauty, for only the guards knew that she was a swimsuit model. All of them were female guards, who, unbeknownst to her, had spiteful envy toward her because of their crush on Shamoney.

"Psss! Psss!"

Shamoney heard an inmate next to him hiss at him. When he turned around, he saw his workout partner, Big Mitch, looking at him while visiting his wife.

"Please tell me that's not Chantele Wilkins from *Swimsuit*."

"Yeah, Mitch, it's her. I forgot to tell you she's my wife," Shamoney informed.

"You lucky son of a bitch!" Big Mitch said as he chuckled. "Hey, me and my wife are going to take pictures in a minute. Can we have her autograph?"

"Can you keep a secret?" Shamoney asked.

"Of course I can."

"Then yeah," Shamoney assented.

When Chantele returned to the table with a variety of food, Shamoney's mouth began to water.

"I didn't know what you wanted, so I got you one of everything. Hope you don't mind."

"Baby, you are good. So how many people noticed you?" he asked.

"None and let's pray that it stays that way. I didn't dye my hair blonde for the hell of it," Chantele said.

"Well, apparently you have a real fan. Big Mitch seems to know you really well."

"Who the hell is Big Mitch?" Chantele wanted to know.

"He's my workout buddy. All he wants is your autograph."

"Are you serious?" Chantele inquired as Shamoney bit into his chicken sandwich.

"Yep!" he retorted while chewing on his sandwich. "Meantime, let's just worry about us. Did you remember how they frisked you when comin' in?"

"Yes, they did a poor job. I could have smuggled a gun in if I wanted to."

"Really?"

"Matter of fact, I brought you something. It's in Shada Jr.'s diaper," Chantele explained.

Shamoney couldn't believe what he was hearing. He had told Chantele that the visit would be the first to just scope out the security before he began to smuggle anything in. Big Mitch was the mule who would suitcase whatever Chantele had brought.

"What did you bring?" Shamoney asked as he picked up Shada Jr. and then sat him back on his lap.

"Just a couple of E pills," Chantele said.

Shamoney dug his finger inside Shada Jr.'s diaper and immediately felt the bundle of pills wrapped in plastic. He looked over at Big Mitch, who was in conversation with his wife, and then at the female CO guards who were too busy talking among themselves.

"Psss! Psss!" Shamoney hissed to get Big Mitch's attention.

"What's up, pal?" Big Mitch answered.

Shamoney quickly and furtively tossed the bundle of E pills to him.

"Get rid of them," Shamoney ordered.

"Sure will do, pal," Mitch replied.

* * *

When Crazy Zoe saw Kenny pull into Taco Bell on US 1 in Stuart, his patience was at zero. "Man, I say we pop both of

28

them now and leave these stankin' niggas at the drive-thru. What's up?" he asked Boxhead, who was a more calm and calculated menace than his hotheaded brother.

"Fuck it! Let's do it. Then we go missing!" Boxhead assented.

Kenny pulled up his nice Lexus SUV to the order box and waited to get served.

"Welcome to Taco Bell, and thank you for choosing us today. May I take your order?" the sexy voice said.

"Man, who that sexy-ass voice belong to?" J-Mack said from the passenger side of the SUV.

"What do you want, J-Mack?" Alexis, the Taco Bell employee asked over the speaker.

"Girl, don't act like you not happy to hear from your crush," said Kenny, who was hanging out the window and never saw the threat approaching, but Alexis did from her monitor.

"J-Mack! Y'all watch!"

Boom! Boom! Boom! Boom! Boom!

"Noo!" Alexis screamed as she watched Crazy Zoe release an entire clip on Kenny and J-Mack, who were caught slipping.

"Shut up, bitch!" Boxhead shouted as he shot at the voice box before he and his brother made their successful getaway.

FIVE

Real pulled up to Jake's store in his new Range Rover with Bellda riding shotgun.

"I won't be long. Just got to holla at V-Money."

"Okay," Bellda replied, changing the Boosie tune to her favorite Monica song.

Bellda watched Real greet all his homies with a dap and then walk inside the store. It was a moment later when Lala pulled up and gave Bellda a sour-ass look.

"Bitch, don't you get fucked up out here," Bellda mouthed to Lala, who read the words escaping her mouth.

Lala impudently stood in front of the Range Rover and shouted, "Bitch, run that mouth out here, ho!"

It was all Bellda needed to hear. She came out of her heels, pulled down her miniskirt, and then hopped out of the Range Rover on go mode. Lala and Bellda clashed, and a blow-for-blow brawl ensued between the two fierce female lions. A crowd quickly formed as the women went at it.

"Oh shit! Somebody go get Real!" Phat Whinny shouted.

When Real stepped outside with a duffel bag full of money, he saw Bellda backing Lala into a corner blow for blow. Unsurprisingly, Lala was hanging in there not yielding to a mad Bellda. Real opened his back door and then tossed the money inside. By the time he made it over to break up the fight, he caught Luscious trying to sneak up on Bellda. Before she could attack, Real grabbed her by the throat and throttled her unconscious. When he let go of her and she hit the ground, Real pulled out his Glock .50, aimed it in the air, and then pulled the trigger.

Boom! Boom! Boom!

The shots startled Lala and Bellda, causing them to pull away from each other. When Bellda saw Real standing there with his gun in hand, she immediately made a dash over to him and tightly hugged him. "Baby, she came out her mouth side."

"Go get in the truck now!" Real sternly demanded.

Without any protest, Bellda did as she was told. He was her man, and what he said ruled.

"Lala, just tell me why?" Real asked a tired Lala panting out of breath.

"Real, she yo' bitch! I don't owe no man but Birdman an explanation!" Lala threw dirt in his face with the obvious understatement.

"Well, tell Birdman to keep his bitch in check or else he'll be eatin' dirt like the rest of these niggas I done bedded. Are we clear?" Real spoke impishly.

"Whatever, man. Like I said, I bow down to no nigga or man. You feel like you king of the streets, nigga. I'm queen of these streets. And if they ain't from 'round here, fuck 'em, nigga!" Lala impudently stood her ground and then stormed off.

As badly as he wanted to grab her around her neck like he had done to Luscious, he let the feisty woman walk away.

Lala helped Luscious to her feet and put her inside her new Mercedes.

"Girl, let's go. I assure you this'll never happen again," Lala promised her fellow Ms. Gorgeous.

"That ho dead anywhere I catch her ass at!" Luscious screamed.

* * *

Back at the mansion, Real showered with Bellda and then tended to all her war wounds.

"I never thought you had it in you like that!" Real exclaimed as he applied the last of the antibiotic ointment on a cut over her eye.

LeLe had come to see about Bellda, but Real ran her off to attend to her himself.

"Well, don't be surprised. I look like a humble soul that wouldn't hurt a fly. But when it's time to get—ouch!" Bellda winced in pain when Real rubbed her cut a little too roughly.

"Sorry, baby," Real retorted as he slowly lay Bellda back on the bed disrobing her from her towel.

Real began planting gentle kisses along her body down to her wet mount. When his tongue swiped across her throbbing clitoris, Bellda moaned and then arched her back. Real removed the towel from around his waist and climbed on top of her, slowly entering her sultry mound.

"Ummm!" Bellda moaned, crossing her legs behind Real's back as he sat in her for a moment.

Bellda could feel every heartbeat of his throbbing dick inside her womb.

"Can you feel that?" he asked.

"Your heart beats in time with mine. My grandmother in Haiti once told me that it's the symbol of real love," Bellda explained.

"There's no doubt that I love you to the moon and back. I respect what you did today, but just know my heart will never betray you. Woman, I love you, and our contentedness is hated by many. You don't have to prove yourself to no one else," Real said before he made slow and passionate love to Bellda.

Lord, I love this man. Please keep him safe! she thought.

* * *

Lala was furious. She didn't have Birdman to lick her wounds like Bellda had posted on Facebook. Birdman was busy trafficking ounces to North Florida for a small-time hustler for V-Money. When Birdman did call and inquire about what was relayed to him, Lala insisted that it was nothing, not wanting to expose what Real had actually told her to relay to Birdman. She simply hung up on him and then ignored his following persistent calls, until he gave up.

"I'ma make that ho eat dirt the first chance I get, I promise," Lala said to herself while taking a soothing shower.

I can't believe I'm going through this bullshit. Girl, pack you and Destiny's shit and get the fuck away from Martin County! Lala's self-conscience prompted her.

"I can't, Lord, I can't!" Lala broke down crying. "I'm in love with a man who don't even love me anymore!"

Lala became weak and collapsed to her knees in the tub, crying uncontrollably as the water cascaded down her body.

"I'ma kill that bitch!" she shouted hysterically.

* * *

"People, we need DEA, ATF, CIA, and FBI. We need everyone to work together as a team!" FBI director Tom Johnson spoke to the overcrowded room of agents from all departments.

"Mr. Mike Stanley was a great agent for many years," Johnson began, showing an enlarged photo of the agent on a massive display screen.

"He was brutally murdered by this mad fucking animal!" Johnson said, changing the photo to a mug shot of Jean Black Pierre.

"People, I don't make threats, I make promises; and I promise that the hard, drudging work will pay off. We can't keep letting this man slip through the cracks. We have his nemesis, Mr. Polo, under surveillance. Now we need to bring Mr. Wilkins under the scope and see what type of fun we will have watching him," Johnson stated as the room exploded in ovation. "We're never running out of time. We are the creators of time, people!" Johnson continued to buoy up the tense agents.

He waited for the crowd to settle down before he spoke again.

"People, we've had a lot on our plates handed to us over this long past year. We have two escapees who are still on the run, and we have diligent agents bustin' their asses on that case alone. Let's keep our eyes open. There has to be someone out there who knows something. I grew up in a rough gutta where snitches came in all forms—gold teeth, dreadlocks, bald heads, and baggy pants. Someone out there knows every answer to our questions. We're going back to the old way of handling things. Pick 'em up and interrogate. DEA, you guys have your suspects, so share them and break them down the old way until we have a solid lead," Director Johnson ordered his agents, who knew exactly what their boss was referring to when he said the "old way."

Director Johnson continued to give out directions as Agent Tod Davis attentively listened. He was feeling what Johnson was instructing. But it didn't matter how many suspects they would beat and torture for information to lead them to Black. It would never amount to the loss of his true friend. He wished that he could find someone in Black's family, but there were many Pierres. A team was being sent to Haiti to see if Black was a stupid man to run home to hide.

I know he's not that stupid. I wouldn't be surprised if the coward was in the same room right now, Davis thought of the prospect of Black's evanescent witness.

<u>SIX</u>

Two Weeks Later

The grand opening of Club 772 was a tremendous success—the best ever recorded along the Treasure Coast. It was also one of the largest clubs, even outdoing the ones in Miami Beach. Real was excited, and the entire Swamp Mafia was present. Not only was it a grand opening for Club 772, but Rick Ross was taking the stage that night with Meek Mills.

Club 772 was a luxurious club with top-dollar VIPs and the best DJ on the Treasure Coast—DJ Pettway—who weighed over four hundred pounds and knew how to keep the club crunk. The place was beautiful and even turned out to be more than what Real himself had expected concerning the striking architecture of the place. He had paid a French architect to put the place together, and he got more than his money's worth. Security was everywhere to make sure things stayed calm.

"Brah, you did it!" Johnny shouted over the crunk club while celebrating in the A-class VIP section with his brother.

Champagne bottles, exotic dancers, and money on the pool table filled the scene. Johnny and Su'Rabbit were feeling themselves, and the club didn't close until 6:00 a.m., so the night was still young.

"No, lil brother. We did it!" Real reminded Johnny as he struck the ball into the right pocket.

Bellda and LeLe were having a splendid time watching Real and T-Gutta get at it on the pool table. They even had their bets going on their men.

"Girl, looks like T-Gutta in trouble!" Bellda shouted over the Boosie hit that stirred the club into a crunk serenade.

"Oh shit! These muthafuckas really 'bout to go ham!" LeLe shouted.

She and Bellda were definitely outdoing every bitch in the club in their matching skintight Alexander McQueen minidresses and fur Raye boots. Around Bellda's neck was a scintillating gold and diamond chunk that read R-E-A-L, letting it be known to whom she belonged.

"Y'all ready for this shit?" DJ Pettway asked the club.

"Hell yeah!"

"Rick Ross!" Pettway introduced as Ross and Meek Mills took the stage to perform.

The crowd went wild when Ross came out with his fat boy swag.

"One time fo' Swamp Mafia," Rick Ross shouted into the mic.

"We about to shake St. Lucie tonight, aye!"

"Hell yeah!" the crowd screamed.

When Real looked at Bellda and caught her looking at him, he winked his eye at her, causing her to blush. He then struck the last colored ball into the pocket, winning yet another game.

"Rack 'em, stack 'em, and then I pack 'em!" Real said to T-Gutta.

"Dirty, you got that. You just ripped me $10,000 in ten straight games. Ain't no getting back for me. I'd be a damn fool!" T-Gutta exclaimed as he downed his last bit of champagne.

"Are you enjoying yourself?" Real asked Bellda.

"Sure! I think we could use your office for a moment. I need to talk to you in private," Bellda shouted into Real's ear.

Real caught on to what Bellda was really inferring. He stuck his arm out and she intertwined hers with it as he said, "Come, my beloved queen. I'm always at your behest."

"Gutta, hold me down. I'll be a moment," Real informed T-Gutta as Juvie, Capo, and Trap Money entered VIP.

"What they do 4-Life?" Real said to Juvie.

"Three hos, one me, baby," Juvie retorted.

"Check it. Stay around here. I need to holla at you and ya brother. I'll return in a moment, feel me?" Real shouted into Juvie's ear.

"Got ya!"

* * *

Lala and the rest of her Ms. Gorgeouses were having a blast in Club 772. However, the fun came to a halt for Lala when she saw Real walking back to his office with Bellda on his arm. It burned her soul to see him with another woman.

That's supposed to be me, Lala thought as Birdman came up from behind her and grabbed hold of her thin waist.

"What's up, baby. You ready to bounce? If not, daddy will be waiting at home until you get there," Birdman said into Lala's ear while pressing his hard-on against her ass.

Lala was feeling the full effects of the Cîroc in her system and was ready to get her groove on with him. But she at least had to see Real one more time, even though she knew it would hurt her.

"Give us about thirty more minutes and we'll leave together," Lala shouted over her shoulders to Birdman.

"Alright, baby," he answered.

* * *

Johnny had his eyes on the gorgeous caramel dancer all night. She was closely and impudently watching him much of the evening as well. He was horny and wanted to gamble his chances of taking her home for the rest of the morning. The club's capacity was slimming as it neared 5:45 a.m.

"I gotta make my move," Johnny encouraged himself.

The dancer was preparing to leave the club and asked the bartender for her last drink, when Johnny came up from behind and sat next to her.

"Whatever she's getting, it's on me," Johnny said to the bartender.

"And who is you?" the exotic dancer shouted back at him over the loud music.

"Just know I'm somebody."

"Oh really?"

"Yeah, and, gorgeous, not being judgmental, I can tell that you are somebody too."

The bartender slid the drink over to her.

"My name is Johnny. People call me Chyna Man," Johnny introduced himself, sticking out his hand.

The dancer took his hand and firmly shook it.

"Courtney Queen," she replied.

"Oh, so you a Queen. Damn! That means we're relatives."

"No, sir!" she said shaking her index finger. "I'm not related to the Queens from Martin. I'm from South Philadelphia."

"Philly, huh?"

"Yes, a Philly Queen!" Courtney said flirtatiously.

"What brings you here?" Johnny asked.

"Business. I dance on call if the money is right. Nothin' more, nothin' less. So, get the mischievousness out of your head!" she warned Johnny.

To his surprise she wasn't a one-night token, but he still was eager to learn more about her.

"Can we talk somewhere that's more quiet than this place?"

"Actually, I was leaving. I have to be in Miami later on today," she said.

"Do you have time for breakfast? I'm paying!" Johnny asked.

Courtney let a moment of contemplative thought go by before she made up her mind. Although she was on a job far off from what she had told him, she had all the time in the world to chill with Johnny Wilkins.

"I guess we could have a nice breakfast. Hey, no fast moves. I'm telling you, I'm not into nothing more than breakfast!" Courtney reminded him.

"Of course, baby. We've already closed that door, right?"

"As long as we're on the same page," she shouted over the music.

"Farewell, club," Johnny said as he let Courtney lead the way.

As Courtney walked in front of him, she did everything in her power to entice his manhood by swaying her delicate hips from side to side. Her body was a banga! And the skintight dress accentuated all her natural curves.

Boy, I might have me a winner! Johnny thought of the prospect of wifey.

But only time would tell what fruits Courtney would produce.

* * *

Detectives Harris and Holmes had shown up to the club hours ago and scoped out the scenery.

"Looks like ya boy Real done raked in more cash in one night than he probably intended to," Det. Holmes informed Harris.

They were sitting in Harris's Tahoe SUV waiting for Real to leave.

"It's 7:45 a.m. I say we just go in and get him," Holmes insisted.

"Nah, it'll scare him to death, and he'll probably scream for his puny lawyer," Det. Harris said sarcastically.

"Speaking of the devils," Holmes said as he was staring at Real and Bellda departing the club hand in hand.

"I swear she could win an Oscar for Best Wife of the Year," Holmes said as Real and Bellda stepped into the backseat of a black limousine.

"Do you remember traffic stops?" Harris asked as he put the Tahoe in gear and then proceeded to trail the limo.

"1952 en route," Harris radioed into dispatch.

"Go ahead, 1952."

"Tag number E-201137 on a black limo," Harris said.

"Ten-four."

While awaiting clearance of the limo's tag, Harris closely trailed them.

Bellda couldn't wait until they made it home. The luxurious confines of the limousine were too much to bypass making love to Real in the backseat.

"Umm, daddy!" she moaned out as Real pounded her from the back.

Her ass was air-bound with her minidress high above her hips.

"Whose pussy is this?" Real asked breathlessly while he stroked her long and rapidly.

"Yours, daddy!" Bellda purred loudly, not caring that the chauffeur was getting an ear full of her love cries behind the private slide.

"I'm coming, daddy. Uhh shit!"

"Arrghhh!" Real grunted as he shot his seed deep inside of Bellda's womb.

When the limousine came to a sudden stop, Real looked around perplexed as to why they were stopping heading south on I-95.

"What the hell are we stopping for?" Real screamed.

When he looked back, he saw that they were being pulled over by unmarkeds. It wasn't until he saw the two familiar detectives emerge from the SUV that he understood that they were being targeted. Before they made it to the driver's side, Real had his lawyer's number on speed dial.

"May I help you?" the chauffer asked politely.

"Yes, sir. Can you let your back window down for us?" Det. Harris requested.

"Is there a problem?" the chauffeur asked.

"Yes, sir. There is. We're looking for a person of interest," Holmes said.

"What's going on, baby?" Bellda asked, frightened and disliking the tone of the female officer's voice.

She knew with all the killing going down that the police could come for Real at any hour.

Lord, please don't take him away from me! Bellda prayed introspectively.

"Let the window down, Chad," Real permitted.

When the window came down, he stared Det. Holmes in her face, but her eyes were not on him. The only person she was interested in was Bellda.

"May we help you?" Real asked.

"Yeah, Bellda Success. We have reason to believe that you have information that could assist us with the investigation of your ex-boyfriend Patron Sinclair."

Oh my gosh!

"Her what?" Real exploded after hearing Pat's name.

"How does it feel sleeping with your enemy's mistress?"

Real's head began to spin. He was not hearing anything Holmes was saying. He couldn't believe his ears.

"Mistress!" he said absentmindedly.

"Real, I can explain!" Bellda retorted as tears flooded her face.

"Ms. Success, could you please step out of the limo and come with us for questioning?"

"But I don't know nothing," Bellda cried.

"You know Patron Sinclair. That's all we need to know," Holmes said as she opened the door and helped Bellda out.

SEVEN

"**P**lease, I stopped seeing Pat. I have no knowledge of nothing that he's done or plotted."

"But you know that he and your new boyfriend are enemies, correct?" Holmes raised her voice at a weeping Bellda in the menacing interrogation room.

For the last two hours, Bellda had been drilled to cough up information that she didn't have. Holmes knew that she honestly did not have any valuable information; however, she knew that everyone slips if correctly pressured.

"Please, Miss, I don't know shit that you are trying to make me know," Bellda cried.

"We're only trying to get to the bottom of a serious matter. A lot of people are dying 'round here, Bellda, and we need more answers. A couple months ago, this lady and her lover were slain," Det. Holmes said, showing Bellda a gruesome photo of Trina Fox and her sugar daddy.

Bellda instantly vomited everywhere when she saw Trina's grisly state of death.

"Please!"

Knock! Knock!

Det. Holmes looked at the door and saw her partner with Real's attorney, Mr. Jordan Wells, a tall, slim white man in his forties dressed in an expensive suit.

"Great!" Holmes stated as they walked through the door.

"Excuse me, I'm here to represent my client, Bellda Success. At this moment, I'm invoking my client's right to remain silent, and I ask that all questioning cease," Mr. Wells spoke with seniority and authority, which prompted an ingenious Bellda to look up. "Is my client free to leave? Are there warrants for her arrest?" Mr. Wells asked.

For a moment, an eerie silence lingered, and Mr. Wells smiled.

"I'll take that as a no. Bellda, come with me. Let's get you home," he said.

The first person Bellda expected to see when walking out of the Martin County Police Station was not there. Instead, her girl LeLe was there with tears in her eyes.

"Girl, are you okay?" LeLe asked, wiping her eyes.

"I feel better. They're trying to make me know something about Pat," Bellda relayed about her two hours of interrogation.

"Well, if you don't know, then you don't know."

"Then they showed me a pic of Trina and how they found her."

"Serious?" LeLe inquired.

"Well, the good thing is they won't be back to talk with you. I don't know their means of messing with you, but if they return, simply say I want my lawyer, okay?" Real's lawyer, Mr. Wells said.

"Yes, sir," Bellda replied to Mr. Wells.

"Bellda, we're going to my house first. We need to talk. Real's not taking this revelation too good."

"Do you blame him?" Bellda said with tears in her eyes.

Before she could break, LeLe embraced her.

"I'll see you ladies around," Mr. Wells said.

"Thank you, Mr. Wells," LeLe answered.

"You're welcome," he said as he stormed off toward his expensive Porsche Carrera GT.

"Let's get you out of here, sis," LeLe said as she walked Bellda over to her BMW SUV.

* * *

Real was heated. He had returned to the mansion, called a U-Haul truck, and immediately packed all of Bellda's belongings. He couldn't believe she had played under him like a duck.

I feel like a stupid, lame nigga. I was a sucka-for-love-ass nigga, to better describe it, he thought.

"She played me like a fuckin' nigga, T-Gutta!" Real said to his friend, who was there for support. "I gave this bitch the world, and she gave me a lie!" Real said as he smashed picture frames and anything else with the two of them on display. "I almost gave this bitch a diamond, T-Gutta!" Real was enraged, shattering another picture frame. "Damn it!"

T-Gutta could understand his pain. He was upset with LeLe because she knew that Bellda was fucking Pat as well.

"She betrayed me, brah," Real said, wiping inevitable tears from his eyes.

With no words, to soothe him, T-Gutta grabbed Real and hugged him in a brotherly manner. Real was unable to bridle his emotions. For the first time since losing his father to the system, he broke down in another man's arms.

"Brah, it's gonna be okay. That nigga is dead, and you've made the right choice by cutting her off. Don't listen to me, brah. Listen to your heart and follow it," T-Gutta suggested.

Damn, I hate to see my nigga like this! T-Gutta thought.

"She betrayed me, brah!" Real cried.

"And you've let her go. It's time to stay focused now. We need you to focus, brah," T-Gutta said.

"Swamp Mafia, my nigga. That's my everything now and forever. Fuck a bitch!" Real shouted as he pulled away from his friend and stormed upstairs.

* * *

When Big Chub pulled up to the curb on Spruce Street in East Stuart, he saw a couple of niggas out who were obviously trapping.

"Crazy Zoe, make a move!" Chub said to him over the walkie-talkie.

Crazy Zoe was in another stolen car coming down the other end of Spruce with his lights off.

"Oh shit! Nigga creeping!" one of the young niggas shouted as he made a dash for his AK-47 in the bushes.

"Get 'em, Boxhead," Big Chub demanded as he dropped the passenger window.

As Crazy Zoe mashed on the gas, Boxhead leaned out the window and pulled the trigger of his M-16, knocking down the foes who had tried to flee.

"Ambush!" one of the men yelled before falling to the bullets of Boxhead's steady shooting.

The five young men slipping up were now dependent on the one with the AK-47 hidden in the bushes to save the day. None of them were older than nineteen. Yet despite their young ages, they were still foes to the Haitian Mafia.

One of them was still breathing and trying to crawl to safety. Crazy Zoe hopped out of the stolen car and came down on an eighteen-year-old known as Kaneboy. He aimed his Glock .40 and emptied the clip into him. Crazy Zoe dropped the clip and inserted another one.

"Haitian mafia, nigga!" Crazy Zoe screamed and then tossed a fresh Haitian flag bandana onto the dead young man.

He then ran into the stolen SUV with Big Chub and his brother, leaving the stolen car that he had driven onto the scene.

"Good job! You two already make Black proud," Big Chub said.

No one saw the see-through drone watching the area in hopes of catching drug activity; instead, it caught a gruesome murder.

* * *

The Haitian restaurant on 179th in Overtown near Miami was packed as usual on a Friday night. The food was delicious and cooked by some of the best chefs from Haiti. It was peaceful and one of Black's top restaurant investments.

Agent Davis stepped inside with his new partner, a gorgeous caramel, five foot six, 135-pound thirty-four-year-old female named Karma Smalls. It was evident to everyone that they were FBI agents by the badges hanging around their necks and exposed firearms on their hips in holsters.

"Crowded place tonight," Agent Smalls said.

"Always on a Friday night," Davis replied.

"May I help you?" a Haitian man asked Davis at the front counter.

"No, sir. We're the FBI, and we're here to see the manager," Davis announced with authority.

"Well, sir, he's not at this restaurant. We have numerous restaurants."

"Don't shit me around, Mr. Baptise. I've seen the other restaurants, okay? Now where the fuck is Mr. Lewis at?" Davis ordered.

The Haitian was indeed Mr. Baptise, and he was stunned that the FBI agent knew exactly who he was. In fact, he was the assistant manager and was running the show, for the most part.

"Come with me, sir," Baptise said as he escorted Davis and Smalls through the restaurant and down a hallway where Mr. Lewis's office was located.

* * *

Palehead from Zo'pound pulled up with his homie, Lil Zoe. They both walked inside the Haitian restaurant.

"Stomach growling, Haitian?" Palehead asked Lil Zoe.

"Smells good," he answered in Creole while approaching the takeout counter.

"Haitian, how may we assist you two young'ins?" an old-school employee asked the men.

"Yeah, um—"

Boc! Boc! Boc!

Shots erupted before Palehead could finish giving his order. The place went crazy, and Lil Zoe was down. Palehead had quickly hopped over the counter and returned defensive fire after pulling out his MAC-10 from under his thick jacket.

Tat! Tat! Tat! Tat!

* * *

Agents Davis and Smalls were in conversation with Mr. Lewis when they heard the fusillade out in the restaurant.

"Those shots are here!" Smalls yelled, pulling out her Glock 21.

"Let's go!" Davis demanded as he took the hallway with his weapon trained on the opening.

Boc! Boc! Boc!

Tat! Tat! Tat! Tat!

As they drew near the main dining room of the restaurant, Davis caught visual of Palehead shooting off his enemies.

"Freeze! Drop the weapon!" Davis commanded as he got down and aimed at Palehead, who was shocked to see the FBI.

"Man, these muthafuckas shoot first," Palehead shouted.

"Put down—!"

Boc! Boc! Boc!

"Cover me!"

"No!" Davis screamed, trying to stop Smalls from pursuing the other gunmen, but she moved too fast and nailed one of them.

Boom! Boom! Boom!

Palehead was adamant about not cooperating, and Davis had a partner to back up.

"Drop the weapon! I warn you," Davis shouted.

Boom! Boom!

Before he could finish warning Palehead, Davis nailed him in the chest with a double tap, causing Palehead to drop his weapon.

He's wearing a vest, Davis thought as he scrambled and kicked Palehead's MAC-10 away from him.

He then joined Smalls in the fusillade that quickly died as the Haitian Mafia Zoes fled in a stolen Dodge Durango.

"Red Durango. 179th locals alert!" Agent Davis screamed into his walkie-talkie for backup from Metro-Dade.

"I got two of them. There's only one in the SUV. I'm going after him until we have good visual," Smalls told Davis.

"No!" Davis screamed again, but Smalls was gone again. "Fuck!" he exclaimed, obviously frustrated by Smalls's adamantine attitude. "This wouldn't be me and Stanley. I'm not used to this shit!" he yelled as he ran back inside the restaurant after Palehead, who was no longer unconscious on the floor.

Palehead had escaped out a back door with no sign of a trail. Davis was furious. "Fuck!" he shouted, having more reason to jump down Smalls's throat when he saw her again.

When he looked around, the only thing he could be grateful for was that only one man was dead. It was evident that Lil Zoe and Palehead were the targets and that they were from Zo'pound, evident from the white and black bandana hanging out of Lil Zoe's pocket. When Davis checked him for a weapon, there were none to be found. The MAC-10 that he had kicked away from Palehead was also now gone.

"Shit!" Davis cursed under his breath as he made a dash to find Mr. Lewis to retrieve the tapes.

But when he got to the office, Mr. Lewis was just another victim who had been shot to death while sitting in his desk chair.

The eerie sight deeply bothered Davis, because Mr. Lewis wasn't shot by Palehead. It was suicide.

* * *

Running red lights at ninety miles per hour was against the locals' protocol, but not the FBI's. Smalls was neck and neck with the driver of the stolen Durango when he sharply turned on 139th. She abruptly braked and followed him. Metro-Dade was safely trailing, following her directions over the walkie-talkie.

Smalls then artistically pursued the Durango, which turned widely onto 123rd and then took a dirt road that curved back into pavement.

"Suspect on 122nd and making a U-turn," Smalls shouted into the walkie-talkie. "What the fuck is he doing making a U-turn?"

She then positioned herself in the middle of the road at an angle as the Durango came back toward her.

She quickly hopped out with her Glock and aimed at the windshield and then fired.

Boom! Boom! Boom! Boom!

The shots shattered the windshield, but the Durango continued at its max.

"He's trying to collide!" she screamed as she continued to round off, simultaneously side-stepping the Durango as it crashed into her unmarked Tahoe Chevy.

The Haitian mafia Zoe came flying through the shattered windshield. The impact was loud, and the dead Zoe flew a number of long yards from the Durango after flying over the hood.

"Son of a bitch just killed himself!" Smalls radioed in.

To make sure, Smalls ran down the road where the Haitian had landed, and never even checked for a pulse. His eyes were wide open with a blank stare of death on his bloody face.

"Damn it! Son of a bitch! Why'd you kill yourself?" Smalls shouted out as she kicked the Zoe's dead body.

This shit is too damn crazy! she thought as Metro-Dade swarmed the area, flooding the streets with red and blue lights.

EIGHT

Death-Struck

When Black received a call from Mr. Lewis that the FBI was in the restaurant and it was under attack, Black informed him that it was best to sacrifice himself to the gods. Because the FBI was there to take him prisoner, Mr. Lewis thoroughly believed Black and took his own life.

Black had just finished having a threesome with the Jamaican twins, Keke and Meme, when he caught the breaking news live on the television. He watched as the FBI agent who had been hunting him for ten years tried to hold off a gun fight between two rivals.

While Black was attentive to the news report, his iPhone rang with a blocked number.

"Hello?" Black spoke in Creole.

"So, we catching each other in the homeland business, Black?" Polo's voice spilled out of the receiver. "Since when we disrespect our own establishments going at each other under Haitian territory, huh?"

"Polo, when was the last time you played by the rules?" Black asked as Meme began sucking his dick to bring him back to life.

Together the twins took turns sucking his dick until he was finally erect.

"Black, you think the gods will respect you disrespecting territory owned by the gods?"

"Listen, Polo, these restaurants belong to me. If my men catch anything from Zo'pound, I order them to take 'em down. You're running out of time, Polo. Who's your sacrifice? Bo-

Bo? If he betrayed me, he'll betray you. Don't you remember anything I've taught you, boy?" Black asked Polo, who was upset that one of Black's men was killed in a Haitian establishment.

"Fuck you, Black! How 'bout I tell you how you will fall. You ever been held up by a young lion? I'ma sit back and watch Chub fall, and then you'll fall by the same lion. Then I'll take over everything with your name on it," Polo reminded Black of his new enemy.

"That young lion is only a pup right now. He don't understand right or wrong. But soon he will understand the power of the gods too," Black retorted.

"Guess who's training that pup, Black?" Polo asked as he began to chuckle. "See, I told you. You're too blind to see your own funeral," Polo said as he disconnected the call, leaving Black in a furious, vagrant, and disturbed mental state as evidenced by his dying erection.

"Leave! You two did good!" Black said as he dismissed the women.

"Call us again, when daddy needs us, okay?" Meme said as she slid into a silk robe.

"Okay, beautiful."

They were gone in no later than a minute.

Polo's last words really disturbed Black. He knew Polo didn't blow smoke. He was too clever to say something that wasn't true or what he was going to do or didn't do.

"So, he's training the pup?" Black mumbled to himself.

You're too blind to see your own funeral! Polo's words taunted Black.

"I will kill the pup myself and then come and kill you, Polo, whether the gods like it or not," Black nonchalantly said to himself, making a lethal mistake by going against the gods.

* * *

After Palehead called Bo-Bo to report the run-in with Haitian men, he was told to report to the secret location where everyone met for important meetings. It was an old, abandoned gym that sat in a very remote area of the Everglades.

When Palehead arrived, Bo-Bo and his entourage were present awaiting his arrival. Palehead was everywhere on the news and had been positively identified by the FBI. He cut his dreadlocks to move furtively, and was now ready to ask Bo-Bo to send word to Polo to have him sent back to Haiti. But Polo strictly had other plans for Palehead, unbeknownst to him.

The only light illuminating the gym came from four burning candles. Palehead entered wearing a black hoodie sweater, and then administered the code handshake with everyone inside.

"Glad you could make it, Palehead," Bo-Bo said.

"Me too, man. Shit crazy out there. I can't believe this shit is happening, man," Palehead spoke in Creole.

"We're all stunned about Lil Zoe's death, but we must not forget that he is in a more peaceful place now, okay?" Bo-Bo said while squeezing Palehead's shoulder for support. "Hold your head up, Palehead, and know that you did what you had to do, Haitian. You did your best." Bo-Bo lifted Palehead's head up by his chin to look him in his eyes. "Polo is proud of you. We will take care of everything. We are a nation, one together." After a slight pause, Bo-Bo then asked, "How much does the Z-Nation owe you, Haitian?"

"The Z-Nation owes me nothing!"

Before Palehead could get out his statement, his Zo'pound brother, Snake, shoved a sword through his back that went through his heart and burst out of his chest. Palehead was dead instantly. Before his knees buckled, Snake pulled the sword out and then swiped at his head, decapitating Palehead with one artistic swipe.

"May the gods bless his soul," Bo-Bo said.

Together, the entourage prayed for Palehead to be in a safe place with their gods.

"Snake, complete the burial. Everyone else, retire back to your own business," Bo-Bo commanded.

All at once, the crowd dispersed and went their separate ways. Further down from the gym was a swamp, which is where Snake dumped Palehead's body, excluding his head.

Snake was a very swarthy, old-school Haitian who had innumerable body counts. With only one eye, he still was able to defeat the best and most fierce fighters and take out the roughest killers. Snake was muscle-bound, stood six two and weighed 225 pounds solid. He was a feared man in the Zo'pound Nation, who knew rituals that would fuck up an enemy's life, despite being limited to specific rituals. The gators came at his call and took Palehead's body under the water.

Polo saw Palehead as a risk since he was wanted by the FBI—people who no doubt would have had him within the next forty-eight hours. The gods had called Palehead home as a sacrifice, a place where he would be at perpetual peace.

* * *

The next morning when Agent Davis arrived at headquarters in Miami, he was still upset with his partner,

Agent Smalls, who he tried chewing out and blaming for Palehead's escape. Director Tom Johnson found that Smalls was simply acting out of duty to her best interest under the perilous situation, and excused her actions.

"Good morning, Davis. Do you want some coffee and donuts?" Agent Smalls offered from her desk at her cubicle.

"No thanks, Ms. Hero," Davis replied sarcastically as he removed his jacket and saw the brown box on his desk.

Looking at the box, his first thought was the footage of the murders from the drone that had occurred in Martin County on Spruce Street.

"I'll handle my own coffee and donuts if I need them," Davis informed Smalls.

"Listen, Davis," Smalls spoke as she stood and turned around to of face him. "Maybe I was wrong in your judgment, but I only wanted to catch the same bad guys. It's neither of our faults that the muthafucka was wearing a damn vest. You even said it yourself that you could tell he had a vest on. So why didn't you cuff him? I didn't raise this hell in front of Johnson, because you're my partner. But before you try to make me feel bad, double check your missed alternatives and cast judgment on yourself. You want to be in your damn feelings. What's done is done, okay? Suck it up, be a man 'bout it, and let's find these muthafuckas. We find Palehead, and we may have our first break," Smalls said as she turned back around and resumed eating her donuts. "And the donut offer is still on the table. I'm not walking to get you coffee now. That offer is gone. I'm mad now!" Smalls added.

"I'll take a donut when I go buy my own, prissy!" Agent Davis said.

"Fuck you, Davis!" Smalls said, getting a chuckle out of her partner.

No, let me fuck you! Davis thought.

Agent Davis read an old report summary about the Martin County prison escape and then stashed it in his file of cold cases. He was a veteran and worked strategically like one. If the suspect wasn't found or there were no convincing evidence-producing leads within forty-eight hours, then the case was considered cold to him. The only case that he refused to accept as cold was Jean Black Pierre.

After sorting through more useless documents, Davis removed a pocket knife from his jeans pockets and cut the sealed tape to the brown box on his desk. When he opened it, he became perplexed when he saw a silver pot inside.

"What the fuck we need with a pot? Are we sure this is ours?"

"Holy fuck! What's that smell?" Smalls shouted, jumping up out of her seat at the reek of bad decomposition.

Agent Davis removed the lid of the pot and got a more intense reek from the gruesome sight of Palehead's decapitated head surrounded by rotten potatoes.

"Agent Smalls, I think we've found Palehead," Davis announced, recognizing the face of the escaped gunman.

"Oh my gosh! I'm about to puke!" Smalls said as she made a dash to the bathroom.

Agent Davis was at a loss for words as he continued to stare at the head. He was searching his vagrant mind for some clue to unbind his bewilderment. Being that Black was Haitian mafia, Mr. Lewis had killed himself, and a Zo'pound man's head was on his desk, Davis suspected no one other than Black.

But why Mr. Lewis? Davis wanted to know.

"Damn, son!" Davis exclaimed loudly.

"Director Johnson is on line one," Agent Smalls said over his shoulder while holding a towel to her nose to avoid the smell of decomposing flesh and death.

* * *

When Real pulled up to Polo's mansion, he greeted Bo-Bo and Snake. After giving them both a dap, he then hopped into the backseat of the limo with Polo.

The chauffeur pulled off, and Polo sparked flame to a phat kush blunt, took a pull, and then passed it to Real. Haitian music emanated at a low volume as they drove through the city limits of East Lauderdale. It was a beautiful sight, and the women were adorable. The limo made a left on 54th and then pulled into a Haitian restaurant that belonged to Polo and was run by a dear friend of his.

They sat at an inside table and enjoyed the delicious meal of curry goat, chicken feet, yellow rice, and fried cabbage.

"Real, you've been a true loyal friend, and I really appreciate you," Polo spoke in a deep Haitian accent.

"Loyalty first. All ready," Real retorted.

"Listen, Real. Zo'pound is bigger than what you see. We are family. We move on cause, and execute risk and failure. The FBI wants me to give up the risk and failure, something Black had already given them," Polo explained to Real, who as always listened attentively. "We are a seasonal fraud master, drug distributor, and vacationer. Since I like you and you're not bound to the rules of Zo'pound, I want to show you how we appreciate you. Zo'pound is moving into the season of vacation that prohibits us from doing anything other than chilling. Real, with your price at 20.5, it's feeble once I give you half of the East Coast."

What the fuck! He say half of the East Coast? Real thought.

"Pablo is a good man, and you've given him the skin off your back and gave me a pure heart. You've outsmarted Black and forced him to give up his own right hand. I'ma give you the secret to kill Black," Polo said as he leaned in closer toward Real while wiping his mouth.

"Kill Big Chub, and Black will surely die. Haitian mafia will yield to Zo'pound when the head falls. He's recruiting every day, son, and you're still a big threat to him. The streets are yours, lion. When Bo-Bo and Snake call you, all you have to do is send your man with whatever and establish yourself. Oh yeah, before I forget," Polo said, reaching his hand into his slacks and retrieving a set of keys, which he tossed in the air to Real.

"What's this?"

"It's a gift from the Z-Nation. It's a nice beach house at 3201 Mango Street in South Beach. It's all yours, and only us two know about it. When you need time to get away, enjoy peace of mind on the beach while staring out at the ocean," Polo said.

"Thanks, Polo," Real answered.

Polo was a real nigga and reminded Real of someone he really needed to go pay a visit. Being engrossed in the streets—killing, dealing, and not chilling—he barely had time for his family and his father. He was going to visit Shamoney for the first time after being cleared.

I gotta go see my father, man.

Polo saw Real lost in his thoughts. He knew exactly what was going through his mind, so he surprised Real when he spoke.

"We only have one father, Real. If you love him, just know he's waiting on you."

What the fuck! This man is too powerful, Real thought. "Can I ask you a question, Polo?"

"Of course."

"Are you a believer of voodooism?" Real asked.

"I am strongly, and it's something I was born in," Polo retorted.

"Is it true that if I don't believe in it, then it won't affect me at all?"

"Real, if you have that much faith in disbelief, then you already believe in it. You're just afraid to trust it," Polo explained.

"Can Black do the works?"

"Yes, he can. That's why it's important to kill Chub. Ineffably, you'll never understand, but trust me, you are protected by Polo gods, whether you believe or not," Polo said.

Real was no fool. He had his skeptical thoughts that maybe Gina was telling the truth about Black casting voodoo on her. Lately, her demented mind had increased to the point that all day she sounded like a chicken if not sedated. Chantele was tired and badly wanted to send Gina off to a mental home. But she first wanted to get approval from Shamoney. She too believed that someone placed a voodoo spell on Gina.

"Black put voodoo on Gina. How can we bring her back?" Real asked.

"Kill Chub, and Black will go weak. He gave Pat to the gods as a sacrifice. Don't let him prevail on you," Polo warned him.

"I won't," Real said.

NINE

Six Months Later

Like Polo had promised Real, his bank, and those of his Swamp Mafia circle were making tremendous numbers. Real moved as a business man, now owning apartment complexes, strip clubs, and more hood stores. So much money was coming his way that he wasted no time in putting it toward investments. The more power he gained, the more ruthless and lethal he became.

The war between him and Black—and Big Chub as second-in-command—became lick for lick. However, Big Chub's impudent wrath was nothing compared to Pat's, since Pat ran from Real's wrath. The local news seemed to stay in the hoods from early in the morning to late at night. Criminal scene investigators were working day and night with the same results—no-witness cold cases after forty-eight hours.

Real hadn't talked to Bellda since moving her out and had been fucking a different bitch every night, dismissing them at the crack of dawn.

Real was the man to know and the young drug lord on the East Coast. He now had state-to-state clients who were trafficking hundreds of kilos from Maine to Florida.

"Yo, Juvie. I need you to handle something for me," Real said to him over the phone while he sat on the back deck of his beach house in Miami.

"What's that, homie?" Juvie inquired.

"I need you to take the ride with Jason up North when they send the four cars back up the way. When business is done, I need Mr. Blake taken care of," Real retorted, orchestrating a hit on one of his client's in New Jersey.

"Say no more, homie," Juvie answered.

"Job well done," Real said as he disconnected the call.

Over the past few months with his beef with Big Chub, Juvie had become close with Real after putting in work for him when he needed a nigga bodied. The streets were his, and he was enjoying the kingly lavishness to the extreme.

Walking back inside his beach house, Real caught sight of his Latina booty call bending over and picking up her clothes. He walked up to her and grabbed her by her phat ass.

Smack!

She let out a soft moan as he slapped her ass.

"Papi not finished with me?" she purred.

"Nah, I still got some business to handle," Real told the gorgeous stripper.

Her name was Sonya, and she knew all the pussy powers to keep Real coming back to Miami just for her. Real picked her up and lay her down on the bed. He then took off his swim shorts and climbed between her legs.

"Fuck me, papi!" Sonya purred. "Uhh yes!" she moaned out loudly when Real plunged deeply into her.

He fucked her long, powerfully, and unmercifully, just like she loved it.

* * *

Despite missing Real, who continued to ignore her, Bellda managed to hold herself together. She was now a shift supervisor at the nursing home, and she had moved into her own plush condo after refusing to move back to her parents' house. She still loved Real and was praying that one day he would call her and take her back. She knew that everyone on the streets was aware that they were no longer together, but she didn't care. Her Facebook status remained "in a relationship." Bellda was on her break sitting out on the patio when Det. Holmes walked up on her.

"You again, huh?" Bellda exclaimed nonchalantly.

"Yep! But I'm not here to tick you off by any means, Bellda," Holmes stated.

"Then what is your means with me?" she stood abruptly, giving Holmes an evil stare.

"Bellda, it's too much killing, and you know who's behind it. He's flooding the streets and coast with poison."

"Listen, what do you take me for? Come on, my job isn't to throw dirt on my man."

"He's not your man any longer, Bellda. We see everything," Holmes reminded her.

"Well, you should know. You're the bitch who—!"

"Another disrespectful insult and I'll arrest you," Holmes shouted.

"Well, I'm done talking to you without my lawyer. Come near me again, and I'll report you to internal affairs," Bellda threatened as she stormed back inside the building.

"Shit!" Holmes exclaimed.

* * *

Johnny was glad to see Courtney again. It had been months of a long-distance relationship with her. She was in town to dance at Club 772, so they could spend time with each other. He knew everything about her and felt like he had known her his whole life. She suggested that they take things slow, for logical reasons: she had been badly hurt in her previous relationship. Johnny couldn't wait to see her.

He was on his way back from Atlanta after dropping off twenty kilos of cocaine to a connect for his brother Real. Despite Real reminding him that he was on the same throne as him, Johnny often felt that he was beneath his brother's feet rather than side by side with him. He was always on the road for Real. Johnny was grateful for himself at times when he heard from Su'Rabbit that a couple of their soldiers were killed.

Every day is another nigga dropping, Johnny thought.

Johnny hadn't realized that he was unlawfully driving over the speed limit until he saw the red and blue lights twirling on the state trooper's car.

"Damn!" Johnny exclaimed.

Once again, he was grateful to be clean. He had nothing but a MAC-10 under his seat. He had no drugs, and his DLs were excellent. He was in Jacksonville at 5:00 p.m., and he still had plenty of time to meet up with Courtney at the hotel before she went to work at the club.

* * *

T-Gutta was in one of his trap houses in East Stuart on Bayou cooking up the last of the twenty-five kilos for Juvie when his iPhone rang.

"Hello?"

"Yo! This shit crazy," Lunatic said.

"What's crazy, brah?" T-Gutta asked his compadre.

"A couple of our niggas just got burned on East Avenue."

"Say what? When?" T-Gutta inquired.

"Just now," Lunatic said.

"Shit! Where are you?" T-Gutta asked.

"I'm pulling up now."

"Come in! We got to get Juvie these twenty-five to put on the cars."

"Yeah," Lunatic said as he hung up.

When Lunatic entered the trap house with his key, the smell of cooked cocaine redolently lingered in the air.

"So, who got hit?"

"Curt, Dirty Green, and Twin. They say the nigga Phat Merk was scared to squeeze and could have saved Dirty Green, but he played like a bitch," Lunatic explained.

"Where Phat Merk at now?" T-Gutta asked, loading two duffel bags, with fifteen in one and ten in the other.

"Say he hit it back to Fort Pierce," Lunatic said.

"So he knows he did something fucked up!" T-Gutta concluded.

"Don't worry. I already got eyes on this nigga. He's in Chyna Man's territory now."

"My nigga, we gonna make an example, straight up," T-Gutta said.

There weren't any workers in the trap house. T-Gutta had come bright and early by himself to start cooking up the coke.

"Let's get this shit to Juvie. Stay behind me," T-Gutta said as he walked out the front door with Lunatic.

T-Gutta stored the duffel bags in the safe box in the .745 and then pulled off on his way to Hobe Sound to meet up with 4-Life's second-in-command.

It was ten minutes later when T-Gutta and Lunatic pulled up on Juvie on a back street in Banner Lake, Hobe Sound.

"What's good, my nigga?" Juvie said.

"Same shit, different day, my nigga," T-Gutta answered.

"That's Tic in the car behind you?" Capo asked.

"Yeah, y'all hear what happened on East Avenue?"

"That shit just hit us. It's crazy. We just seen Dirty Green last night out here fucking with Trap Money," Capo said.

"Well, you know how these streets go. We in one minute, and we gone the next!" T-Gutta exclaimed.

A minute later, a tow truck with three Toyotas on the bed pulled up to Juvie and Capo's trap house and pulled into the backyard. Real's cousin Coy hopped out and walked back up front to meet T-Gutta.

"Y'all ready to do this?" Coy said.

Coy was from the swamp and owned his own towing company. He trafficked kilos up the road for Real, which were stashed inside the cars.

"Let's handle this shit!" T-Gutta said as he walked to his .745, unloaded the safe box, and safely stashed the duffel bag in one of the trucks.

"Alright, y'all niggas get there safe and back," T-Gutta said to Coy and Juvie, who gave him the thumbs up and then pulled off.

"So, Capo, what's really good?" T-Gutta asked his friend, who had sparked flame to a kush blunt.

"Like everybody, just out here trying to make a killing and doing just that," Capo answered.

"It's always enough for all of us out here, brah. If a nigga tells you different, tell them niggas or that nigga to come see me, dirty," T-Gutta informed Capo.

"I will, brah!"

"Yo, Gutta, you good?" Lunatic shouted.

"Yeah, brah. I'm cool."

"I'm out," Lunatic retorted as he pulled off to go handle some much-needed business.

* * *

Big Chub was relaxing in his thirty-foot, uniquely designed backyard pool at his beautiful home in Delray Beach. It was straight Haitian mafia territory from 6th Street to 12th Street. His iPhone rang on the edge of the pool. He swam over to the edge and then answered the call. "Hello?"

"Nephew, is everything good?" Black asked in Creole.

"I have a couple niggas laying in the strip club tonight. Seeing if I could bring the coward to daylight, unc," Big Chub informed Black.

"Good move, nephew. I wouldn't have thought of that," Black admitted. "I want you to hit two of them, and a lot out for the count. It's time to go national. He has no choice but to show his face," Black instructed Chub.

"I got you, unc!" Big Chub retorted, already feeling his adrenaline from the smell of slaughter.

"I know you do, nephew," Black said as he ended the call.

Big Chub immediately called up Crazy Zoe.

"Yeah!"

"Find Boxhead and meet me at the trap on 6th," Big Chub commanded Crazy Zoe before hanging up the phone.

* * *

It wasn't long before Lunatic caught up with Phat Merk. He waited until he saw him walk to the corner store on Avenue E.

"What's up, Phat Merk?" Lunatic spoke as he pulled up alongside him.

The look in Phat Merk's eyes revealed his fear of seeing Lunatic. He had come to Fort Pierce City to lay low.

"Damn! What, what's up Tic?" Phat Merk stuttered.

"I need to holla at ya. Hop in the car," Lunatic asked.

"I can't right now!"

"Nigga, get yo' phat ass in this car!" Lunatic barked.

Phat Merk weighed every bit of three hundred pounds. When he tried to run and reach for his gun under his gut, Lunatic raised his MAC-10 from his lap and filled his protruding belly with hot lead. When Phat Merk hit the ground still breathing, Lunatic stepped out of the car and emptied a clip into him. He then hopped back into his car, leaving Merk dead on the sidewalk.

Lunatic wasn't going to wait until T-Gutta made up his mind to go get Phat Merk, especially when he knew where to find him. Phat Merk had fucked up.

Being a bitch when it's time to be a soldier isn't anyone's backbone or brother's keeper, Lunatic thought as he hopped on I-95 and headed back to the swamp.

TEN

Club 772 was crowded beyond capacity as usual. Real and the Swamp Mafia were in the first-class VIP section enjoying the pleasure of exotic dancers and the crunk music that DJ Pettway perfected. Chantele was hanging out with Real until Bellda and LeLe showed up and stole her away. Seeing Bellda looking as gorgeous as always hurt Real. Despite the fact that he had continued to ignore her and fuck other women, he still had love in his heart for her.

"V-Money, I'll be in my office if y'all need me. I gotta handle something," Real shouted to him.

"I got you!" V-Money yelled back while dancing with an exotic dancer.

"Yo, Johnny!" Real called out as he passed by his brother, who was dancing with Courtney.

"Yeah?"

"You got a bad one. You been dancing with her all night."

"That's because she is mine," Johnny retorted. "Meet Courtney. Courtney, this is my big brother Real I've been telling 'bout," Johnny introduced.

"So, I finally get to meet the man of the building. For months, I couldn't find you."

"I'm a very busy man, ma. It's a pleasure to meet you too. Take care of my baby brother, okay?" Real said to her, squeezing her shoulders before proceeding to his office.

When Real entered his office, he sat behind his ornate desk and rubbed his temples. Seeing Bellda after months of avoiding her really stressed him out.

She lied to me all along. She knew exactly where to find this nigga. Gina wouldn't be a demented woman had I gotten to Pat myself, Real thought as he pulled up the club's cameras on his computer and found Bellda having a splendid time with Chantele and LeLe.

Although Bellda looked joyful, Real could still see that she was a battered woman on the inside. He badly wanted to go out and grab her, but he knew that his ego was too macho to submit to how she had left him in the bind. When Real looked at the east wing camera, he saw Lala and Birdman having the time of their lives. Real smiled at the prospect of the two women who had broken his heart in the same vicinity.

"Life just ain't right sometimes," Real said.

Real picked up his iPhone from the desk and called around checking on his three strip clubs that he owned in Martin, St. Lucie, and Palm Beach Counties.

"Hello?" Var answered. He was the manager at the Coconut Grove Strip Club in Martin County.

"Everything good?" Real inquired.

"Everything is wonderful. Money is piling to the roof in this bitch tonight. A bitch named Roxy is killing the players' pockets. Stop by when you get a chance," Var said to Real.

"I'll do that. I'ma swerve through in a couple hours."

"I'll be waiting, and Roxy too," Var said.

"Oh yeah? She down for the extra mile?" Real inquired.

"Most definitely. The bitch is bad, and she 'bout her money, brah!" Var added.

"Keep her there until I get there," Real commanded as he hung up the phone.

* * *

The two six foot four, 225-pound bodyguards standing at the front door of BodyTalk were taken by surprise when the slugs pierced through their chests.

Boom! Boom! Boom! Boom!

Crazy Zoe and Boxhead entered the club with two Glock .40s each and began dropping everyone in their path.

Boom! Boom! Boom!

They wore ski masks over their faces to avoid the national news. Crazy Zoe made a dash toward the DJ booth and nailed the DJ twice in the head. The strip club was a wild stampede. People were desperately trying to evade the mass shooting. Some were more fortunate than others. Crazy Zoe hopped on top of the bar counter and dropped two empty clips, and then quickly and artistically inserted two fresh clips. When he looked back at his brother, who was adding more bodies to the count, he saw the manager creeping with a double-barrel pump. Crazy Zoe aimed past his brother and took down the manager, who was a white man from New York hired by Real.

"Let's go!" Crazy Zoe exclaimed as he made a dash for the front door.

Big Chub was outside and initiated a fusillade, leaving more bodies by the works of his AK-47 rifle.

Chop! Chop! Chop! Chop!

Crazy Zoe and Boxhead came out squeezing until they safely made it to their getaway car.

Big Chub hopped into the driver's seat and burned rubber, leaving behind the grisly mass killing.

* * *

While Club BodyTalk was being raided, two of Big Chub's assassins were piling up the body count at Club Snow

White in Palm Beach County. Lunatic happened to be there and surprised both men. He took them out in the parking lot as they tried to make their escape. When Palm Beach County Police made it to the club, Lunatic surrendered his weapons and was taken down for questioning.

* * *

The news prompted Real to shut down Coconut Grove and be on standby. With help from the authorities, Var quickly informed everyone of the threat.

"I can't believe this shit!" Real shouted in rage in the Coconut Grove office.

Var himself was ready to find Big Chub and send him to his maker. Real had a lot of weight on his shoulders. Families were grieving and reprehensibly blaming Var.

"Man, that nigga trying to pull you in the open," Johnny said to Real, who was sitting on the edge of Var's desk.

"Well, if that's what he wants, then we gonna give it to him. Lunatic will be released. Mr. Wells is on his way to get him now. Johnny, I need everyone at the trap in an hour. We 'bout to turn up the heat on this shit!" Real said as he stormed out of the office with Juvie on speed dial.

He had a plan formulating in his head.

Big Chub had finally slipped up and allowed me access to his castle. I'm a wise man and a real chess player, Real thought.

* * *

"So, you're telling me that Real isn't your boss, huh?" Det. Harris asked Lunatic.

As soon as Palm Beach called Martin County's office to inform them that they had brought in Alfred Jones Jr. (a.k.a. Lunatic), detectives Harris and Holmes hurried over to interrogate him.

It was hard for them to catch Real on anything. Over the past few months, not even a fiend would agree to set up Real's organization to help bring him down. They were meritless of their speculations of Real's involvement with drugs, murder, and conspiracy.

"Man, listen to me. I'ma tell y'all like this. I don't know who this Real cat is."

"Stop pulling my leg. He's your fuckin' childhood buddy," Holmes shouted.

"Woman, yo' period must be on," Lunatic said to a heated and frustrated Holmes.

"Mr. Jones, I'ma tell you like this. You will go down with him when we get Real. We know what's going on. Remember that, okay?" Det. Harris said to Lunatic as he walked out of the interrogation room with his partner.

"This is crazy. Everyone protects him like a damn god!" Holmes expressed as they walked to the parking lot.

"Don't let it stress you out. We're going to take 'em all down before the year is out," Harris said as he climbed into his unmarked car.

"Great!" Holmes exclaimed, slapping her hand on her right thigh and looking at her phone.

She had a text from the chief of police, Richard Cummings, that informed her to get together with the FBI.

"He's telling us to get with the FBI," she told Harris.

"Yeah, great! That man is obsessed with Haitians."

"Can't blame him. He's been hunting the man for ten years nonstop," Harris added as he merged into traffic.

* * *

Big Chub was highly disappointed in his two hit men who had failed their mission. Their names were Haitian Boy and Jean. Their government names were released, and now the entire world knew who they were and where they were from.

"I can't believe they let buddy get off on them," Crazy Zoe said from Chub's den.

"It's not good! Police will be in the hood investigating everybody. Make sure you let these niggas know to keep their mouths closed or pay in death," Big Chub demanded from Crazy Zoe.

"I'm already on it, Chub. These niggas already know to keep their mouths closed," Boxhead said.

"In a couple days, when shit gets secured, we go to Miami for a couple weeks to let shit calm down," Big Chub said as he walked upstairs to go check in with Black, who—like everyone else in the world—was watching the breaking news.

* * *

Port au Prince, Haiti

Grandma Benita was at her table reciting her ritual in Creole. She and Black were sitting nude in throne-like chairs. Around her neck was a necklace made of bloody chicken and pigeon bones. He was lost in her spell, which revealed to him the danger ahead of him.

"A strong man will be too much for you to defeat by yourself. To recruit later opposed to now will surely cause your enemy to advance on you. Black, the gods are upset with you. I see your nemesis, Polo, laughing. When you fall down the dry well alone, you will be left to die, and no one will hear you cry. Black! Black! Ol' Haitian Black! Recruit! Recruit!" Grandma Benita chanted while throwing a dead man's ashes on Black, who was still hypnotized in a deep trance, seeing all that Grandma Benita was showing him in her spell.

Black's eyes rolled to the back of his head as his body began to convulse and white foam shot from his mouth.

"Black, recruit or die! Recruit or die!" Grandma Benita continued to chant, circling Black in the throne.

"Recruit, Black, or you shall surely die!"

* * *

Juvie and Coy had just crossed the Georgia line when Real called Juvie and told him to abort the mission. Juvie hopped in one of the Toyotas and traveled back to Martin County.

"Yo, Trap Money, y'all niggas be in position when I come through," Juvie said into his phone.

"I got ya, brah. I'ma find Capo's ass now," Trap Money said.

When Juvie ended the call, he put the Toyota on cruise control and respectfully obeyed the speed limit. He was fortunate to still be in Florida when Real had called.

"Damn! This shit getting mo' real every day!" Juvie said to himself.

* * *

Real had spotted the unmarked car lights. He was in his new black-on-black Maserati Ghibli Q4.

"I swear, these muthafuckas just don't give up, huh?" Real said as he turned left on Indian Street and made a sharp left into the Hess gas station.

The unmarked SUV followed suit. Real pulled up to gas pump 11 as the SUV pulled behind him. Stepping out of his Maserati, Real shook his head and then walked around to the rear. He leaned against it and crossed his arms while waiting for the occupants of the car following him to step out.

When detectives Harris and Holmes stepped out, Real was not at all surprised. As they walked toward him, Harris removed his sun shades.

"This is a nice one, Jermaine, or should I call you Real?"

"I think we should call him Lord of the Mayhem," Holmes interrupted.

"Well, let me call you and yo' partner some desperate cunts. Why do y'all persist in trying to make me the bad guy, huh?"

"Because just like everyone else who knows, you're a cold-blooded animal who don't give a shit about no one's safety but yourself," Holmes exploded, getting in Real's face. "Let me tell you something, Mr. Jermaine Wilkins. You could play the innocent role all you want, but your day in hell will be here soon. We know you killed Trina Fox, and we know why. We see everything, and I mean everything. Sooner or later not even all the money you put into Mr. Wells's hands to represent you will bring you home. Your father, Rob Bass, thought he could outmaneuver the law too. Now his dumb ass is doing life. And we'll have you, and death row will be pushed thoroughly," Holmes said, then turned on her heels with Harris.

Before Harris hopped back into the driver's seat, he stood up in the doorway.

"Nice sports car. It'll go good at the auction."

"Same as your house if you come near me again," Real retorted as Det. Harris broke out with an impish chuckle.

"I'll admit, son, you've risen to some stronghold of power, but you're not that powerful," Harris said as he got into the SUV and drove off, praying that he wouldn't have to eat his words.

Real hopped back into his car and pulled off as well. Now that they were off his trail, he could proceed with his intentions. He had a long-time friend named Guin who worked for the Martin County Sheriff's Department in road patrol. He urgently needed to see Guin, who was waiting for his arrival.

When Real pulled up to the luxurious home with the nicely manicured lawn, he saw Guin opening his garage door and waving him to pull his Maserati inside. Guin closed the door and then stared at the car in awe.

"Damn, man! Did you have to bring your best?" Guin asked.

Guin stood six four and weighed 225 pounds of solid muscle. He loved to lift weights and eat protein bars all day. Real and Guin had been down since grade school. He was the second realest white boy that Real had loved like a brother, other than Kentucky.

"This looks like my best? I wonder what my worst looks like. Shit! I know a nigga eatin', but a 'Rati is just a 'Rati! I'm thinking 'bout getting myself a Royce," Real explained.

"When you do, prepare yourself for the feds to really come snooping around!" Guin warned as he walked off. "Come inside."

"Feds or locals can kiss my ass. Guin, you know I ain't going back," Real stated as they walked through the door that led them into a spacious kitchen.

"Care for a beer?" Guin asked as he dug inside the refrigerator and grabbed two cold Budweisers.

"Care for a blunt?" Real asked, catching the Budweiser that Guin tossed over to him.

"Shit! Why not?" Guin retorted. "Come," he said as he led Real to his study.

"Damn! This your office? This bitch is a mini-apartment," Real exclaimed, checking out the opulence of the study.

Real sat in the leather La-Z-Boy chair and pulled out a phat-ass dro blunt. "We smoking in here?"

"Yeah, fire that muthafucka up!" Guin insisted as he sat down at his desk and booted up his computer. "Where we looking?"

"Palm Beach. My boy nailed two assassins. They were both locals, and I need their and their kin's info," Real explained as Guin keyed away on the computer.

He pulled up the mass club shooting where detectives were still on the scene.

"Here," Real said as he tossed the blunt in the air to Guin.

Guin caught the blunt and then inhaled deeply while still keying away.

"DMV has one of the assassin's addresses as 1209 6th Street," Guin informed while scrolling down with the mouse. "The other one is on 8th Street. Both are from Delray Beach. Come see for yourself."

"I don't need to. I believe you, brah. Now stop sleeping with the blunt. Puff, puff, and then pass, nigga!" Real said while texting the information to Juvie, who was still on the road heading back to Martin County.

"The second one is 2012 8th, pal, by the way," Guin added.

"It doesn't matter. Thanks, brah!" Real retorted.

ELEVEN

Pulling up to the dope hole on 6th Street in Delray Beach, the fiend driver stopped in front of five Haitians hanging out and sitting on a brick sidewalk wall.

"Nephew, I need a twenty!" the fiend ordered.

He was driving a stolen Dodge cable van dressed in stinky, oily clothing. Everything about him screamed "fiend." His name was Haitian George, and he was from downtown West Palm Beach.

"Who you, Haitian?" one of the Haitian men asked him.

They were Haitian mafia Zoes, evident from the bandanas tied around their necks. Behind the wall, unbeknownst to George, were three AK-47 rifles loaded and ready. All at once the Haitian men rushed the van with crack rocks in their hands on display.

"Buy my shit. His dope is fake!" the others screamed about the other dopers while trying to down-talk the next man's products.

In all actuality, they all had the same product from the same drop. Leaving their AK-47s behind was a mistake. The fiend purposely tapped the horn and made it look like an accident. The Haitians were so rowdy that they never heard the back doors open. All they saw was fire from the barrel of Juvie's AK-47.

Chop! Chop! Chop! Chop!

T-Gutta jumped out behind Juvie, and Real was right behind T-Gutta. Together they chopped down all but two Haitians, who only suffered gunshot wounds to their legs. Real grabbed one of them by his long dreads and dragged him to the back of the van while Juvie and T-Gutta grabbed the other man. Once secured, Real and T-Gutta jogged down the road until Lunatic pulled out a cut in a stolen SUV while Juvie hopped inside with the fiend.

* * *

When Big Chub heard about what occurred on 6th Street, he became furious and extremely paranoid. He had no clue if his enemy had killed his men or if it was some random beef among the other hoods. He had Crazy Zoe and Boxhead out gathering information. They were also furious after learning that one of the slain Haitians was their cousin. Big Chub refused to accept that the killing was a coincidence. In the core of his gut, he felt that Real was responsible.

"So, what you think, unc?" Chub asked Black over the phone.

"I think it's him. We'll have to sit back and see if he owns up to it. Then we'll go from there. Meantime, I need you in Miami," Black recommended.

"What about Crazy and them?" Big Chub inquired.

"Leave them, and let them hold the folks down. We need them to be on deck if it is Real, nephew," Black informed Chub.

I see what he's doing now, Big Chub thought, after looking at the overall picture.

Black knew that it was Real who had killed their men, and he was now protecting his most powerful piece to the game to prevent him from vulnerability.

"I'll be down in an hour, unc!" Big Chub said to Black before he hung up.

* * *

Black could tell that Big Chub was upset about having to come to Miami. He knew that he wanted to return the favor to Real and go on a tit-for-tat slaughter. But life was not checkers; it was much more like chess. Contemplate your move five moves ahead. Real had found access to Chub's front door, so it wouldn't be long before Real's wrath came down on him. So to prevent the fall from his power piece, Black had to make a power move himself—a move that would keep him in the game.

"Real, you'll never take a veteran out of the game," Black stated while sitting alone in his office.

He was looking at a beautiful woman. She was a Haitian who he had made a part of his life since learning of her dealings with his enemy. Her name was Bellda, and she was a sacrifice.

* * *

Ms. Addie had to step out to use the bathroom. As she neared, she heard soft moans escaping the master bedroom. It was the cries of sweet lovemaking.

Damn, woman! It sounds like it's good! Ms. Addie thought.

She walked into the bathroom and the moans intensified.

"Shit, 'Money, I love you! Oh, daddy. Yes, I'm coming!" Chantele moaned.

"Good Lord, child," Ms. Addie exclaimed as she flushed the toilet.

When Ms. Addie walked out of the bathroom and down the hall, she saw that the master bedroom door was ajar. Being nosey, she peeked inside the room and saw Chantele lying on her bed with her eyes closed and softly moaning while fucking herself with a dildo.

"Mmm! Mmm!" Chantele moaned.

The sight of Chantele pleasing herself caused Ms. Addie's juices to stir between her legs. She wanted to join Chantele and introduce her to an old-school lesbian vet.

"Lord, let me go. That woman is married. At least she's not fucking another man on her husband," Ms. Addie mumbled to herself as she hurriedly walked away from the door and back to her room with Gina.

* * *

It was three o'clock when Johnny's iPhone woke him from a deep sleep. He looked over while feeling for Courtney, and saw that she was gone. The room was completely dark. The only illumination came from his phone.

"Hello?" he answered.

"Damn, nigga! Where you at, on vacation?" Su'Rabbit's voice boomed through the speaker.

"Shit!" Johnny exclaimed, realizing that he was supposed to be somewhere with Su'Rabbit. He had forty bricks of cocaine to pick up and ship to Atlanta. "My bad, brah! Shit! I fell asleep. Where you at?" Johnny inquired.

"I'm at the slaughter pad, and we have company. Get here. Real's waiting too," Su' said before hanging up.

Damn! How the fuck did I fall asleep? Last thing I can remember is me and Courtney watching Empire, Johnny thought, rubbing his throbbing temple.

He had a slight headache and a dry mouth like he had been popping pills all night. But that wasn't the case, because all he did was smoke kush and drink liquor.

"Courtney!" he called out for his beautiful girlfriend, with whom he was taking it slow. He thought tonight would be the night to break her in, but she insisted that they wait until after her thirty-fifth birthday the following week. "Courtney, where are you?" Johnny screamed with a dry throat. When he stood up, the entire room began to spin. "Damn! What the fuck is going on?" Johnny asked through blurry vision.

"Baby, are you okay?" Courtney said as she came into the dark room.

Johnny couldn't see anything. While feeling the wall for the switch, he felt Courtney's hand instead grab his, put it behind his back, and slap on a pair of handcuffs.

"Girl, what you up to? None of that kinky shit now," Johnny said with a smirk on his face.

"Where's the slaughter pad at, Johnny?" a male voice asked.

"What the fuck? Who in my shit, Courtney?" Johnny asked, afraid and perplexed.

"The FBI, Mr. Chyna Man," Courtney's voice boomed back.

"You're under arrest unless you convince us," FBI Agent Smalls said to him as she led him out of the room and outside his mini mansion, with Agent Davis on her heels.

"What the fuck is going on, Courtney?" Johnny asked as he jerked away from Smalls and ran into a big fist that knocked him out cold.

"I told you the fucka would act stupid, Courtney," Agent Davis said sarcastically.

"My name's not Courtney to you, jackass!" Agent Smalls corrected.

"Sorry, I didn't mean to upset you, partner," Davis said as he tossed Johnny into the backseat of their unmarked SUV.

"Fuck you, Davis."

"When?" Davis slipped and said aloud.

"What did you just say?" Smalls asked, surprised and not believing her ears.

"Win. W-I-N!" Davis clearly emphasized.

"I thought that's what I heard," Smalls said with a blushing smirk on her face.

Cracka, you wouldn't know what to do with this pussy. I heard yo' slick ass, Smalls thought, before actually thinking of the prospect of being with Davis.

She had a thing for white men while growing up in the suburbs of Washington, DC—and not in Philadelphia, where she told Johnny she was from. As they drove to their headquarters in Martin County, Smalls broke the ice, regretting it immediately.

"So, where's your sweetheart, if you don't mind me asking?"

"Why is it relevant?" Davis asked, feeling uncomfortable with Smalls snooping into his private and personal life.

"Because I know what you said back there," Smalls retorted, with an impish smile on her face.

Good girl gone bad, Davis thought.

"Whatever!" Smalls stated as she turned away from Davis and stared out the window. "Forget that I asked," she said, keeping their relationship professional.

"It's okay. She died years ago. We were only engaged when Black's men killed her," Davis explained, dropping a bomb on Smalls, who had no idea of his loss.

"Sorry to hear that, Davis," she said sympathetically, feeling the pain for him.

"It's okay. I just want to catch this bastard and kill him myself. I owe her that much."

"That's why you won't let Johnson remove you from the case, even after losing Stanley?" Smalls asked.

"Would you run from the man who stole your heart, or make him pay drastically?" Davis asked, looking Smalls in her eyes as he came to the red light at an intersection.

"You have no intentions of letting him live when you do catch him, do you?" Smalls asked a question, avoiding having to answer his question.

"Would you run from him or make him pay?" Davis asked again persistently.

Smalls thought for a moment in silence, looking Davis in his elegant blue eyes. To be in his mid-fifties, Smalls saw that he was stunningly handsome, something she had never seen in him before. She smiled before veraciously responding, "Yes, Tod, I would kill him with a bullet between his eyes. And I'm here to help you conquer your goal, Tod. You can trust me, okay?" Smalls said sexily.

"Now that's my type of woman," Davis retorted.

"I thought it was big women," Smalls joked.

Regaining his consciousness, all Johnny could do was hate himself for letting down his guard. He couldn't believe how he had let Courtney get under him.

This bitch no doubt knows everything about me and my brothers. They are feds, and when the alphabet boys pick you up, they have 100 percent of their case already laid out, he thought. *Damn, man! How did I slip?*

Johnny was furious, and he could only stare at the back of Courtney's head through the cage that separated them.

* * *

Su'Rabbit had skinned both legs of the Haitian named Zo'Papi as if he were a wild animal being prepared for cooking. Su' was having a field day with the filet knife, pumping the Haitian for information. The second Haitian who refused to cooperate died a soldier with a bullet to his head. However, Real, T-Gutta, and Juvie were enjoying the sight of Su'Rabbit's torture.

"Please! I give you everything!" Zo'Papi shouted in devastating pain when Su' peeled another strip of skin from his upper thigh to his knee. "Ahhh! Please kill me now!"

"Shut the fuck up!" Su'Rabbit retorted as he peeled off another strip of skin on Zo'Papi.

"I think we have everything, Su'Rabbit," Real said while looking at his Rolex.

Where the fuck is Johnny? Real thought, seeing that it was almost 4:45.

"Su', tell me something. Did Johnny say that he had to do something?" Real asked.

"Nah, but that nigga sounded torn the fuck up, you know. He retired earlier today, and told me that he would be out when it was time to load up," Su'Rabbit relayed to Real.

"T-Gutta and Juvie, y'all go load up," Real said, looking at his watch again. "We need to get these bricks to St. Pete before noon, man. Johnny just gotta sit this one out. My man is waiting on me."

Real had a big-time connect in St. Pete, named Brent, who was copping serious quantities of cocaine and had the streets of St. Pete on lock.

"Su'Rabbit, brand his ass and take him back home," Real instructed as he left the slaughterhouse.

* * *

As the men piled out of the warehouse, Agent Smalls snapped away on her high-tech Cannon digital camera, picking up three hundred yards of distance. She was photographing Jermaine Wilkins (Real), head of the Swamp Mafia; Travon Jamison (T-Gutta), his lieutenant; and Markee Anderson (Juvie).

"So, this is the slaughter house, huh?" Smalls asked Johnny, after snapping more pictures of Real's Maserati leaving the warehouse in a hurry.

"Yeah, this is the slaughter house," Johnny said sadly as he dropped his head with a lost feeling of dignity.

He was ashamed of himself for going against the code.

"We have Mr. Jermaine 'Real' Wilkins, but we need more than a body. Do you understand, Mr. Chyna Man?" Davis asked Johnny.

"Yeah, I got you."

"Alpha one, move in," Davis said on his mic to the rescue takedown team of agents who had surrounded the place.

"Ten-four," an agent responded.

* * *

Su'Rabbit had just finished carving the words Swamp Mafia into the back of Zo'Papi when the door came down and a swarm of FBI agents entered the warehouse. Fortunately, he was near his AR-15, and instinctively grabbed it and squeezed off a couple shots before his body was filled with M-16 slugs.

He managed to take out three agents, hitting them all in the head.

"Cease your action!" an agent screamed to a dead Su'Rabbit as he slid down the wall with stagnant eyes.

"Suspect down by agent restraint. Pronounced dead," an agent said into his earpiece as he stared at Su'Rabbit, who had died with a smile on his face.

When Johnny heard the call after the shots, a tear fell down the right side of his face. He only had one tear left for a friend he had betrayed and caused to die a soldier.

Lord, help my soul! Johnny introspectively prayed to the Almighty.

TWELVE

It didn't take long for the news of Su'Rabbit's death to hit the streets and shake the coast. Real went into a wild, frenetic state and commanded his lieutenants, T-Gutta and V-Money, to close down shop at all the trap houses.

They were moving as if it was a drought. Juvie and Coy were already on the road going north with five cars on the bed of the tow truck, with each car filled with fifty kilos. There was no reason to stop them, but Real did prompt them to keep their eyes open. If they saw anything amiss, Juvie was to take down the threat.

The Swamp Mafia circle was gathered at Real's palace in the den trying to figure out what the hell went wrong. The slaughter house was low key. If the feds had moved in on him, that meant there was a snitch or the feds had been watching him.

And if they are watching me, they are watching Johnny as well, Real thought. "Johnny says when he did show up, he saw the feds everywhere," Real told the group.

"Why didn't he call nobody?" V-Money interrupted Real.

"He says he left his phone rushing to get out of there," Real retorted, feeling like he was backing up his brother with an explanation. Yet he couldn't explain the eerie feeling he had.

"Do you think they watched Johnny?" Var asked.

"That was his role, dawg. It would be stupid for us not to think that they weren't," Real said.

After speaking with Real, Johnny went to lay low at his bitch Dominique's house in Fort Pierce City. Everyone knew that the block was hot, and it was prudent for everyone to lay low.

"Listen, shop is closed for three weeks, and I want everyone to lay low. I'm about to skip town. When I get back and everything is good, we'll open back up. Until then, it's drought. At the same time, y'all niggas need to keep yo' ears to the street. Phat Whinny, shut down shop in Okeechobee too. It's a drought."

"I got ya, brah," Phat Whinny replied.

"Bruna, shut down the shop. If the feds are watching, we'll see them before they see us," Real paused as he then looked at the faces in the room for any snake aura.

He saw none. The only two faces he couldn't see were his own flesh and blood, Shamoney and Johnny. He didn't need to check them. Real knew his siblings better than anyone in the room.

They are like me—thoroughbreds, Real thought.

"Because that's all we gonna be doing is watching for them, my niggas. We dismissed," Real said as he stormed upstairs to pack a bag for a small vacation.

Kentucky would be waiting for him to land in Mexico in a few hours.

Once everyone left their separate ways and Real had packed his bags, he called Johnny and relayed to him the same thing he had told everyone else. Real could tell that Johnny was hurt by losing his close friend, from the emotion in his voice.

"Man, lil brah, we all feel your pain. We all out there and all living by the gun. So if the gun does take us, we knew any day that it could. Grieve today, but smile for yo' nigga and our homie tomorrow," Real said to Johnny over the phone.

"Thanks, brah! Without you, I'd be on some stupid shit," Johnny retorted.

"I'm glad you're not. I'm gonna see Mom and Precious, and then I'm out."

"Mexico, huh?" Johnny checked for assurance.

"Yeah, Mexico. I got a friend waiting—"

Real stopped talking when his phone died. He didn't have time to recharge his phone earlier in the day, and the battery was now dead. He simply needed to see his mom and sister and then get out of Martin County and the country altogether.

"I'll charge this bitch on the plane," Real said as he tossed a duffel bag over his shoulder and grabbed any other one he could find. He planned to look less like he was wealthy and more like a normal fly-ass nigga from out of state going wild in Mexico.

* * *

"I wonder who the hell is in Mexico. Do you think it's his connect? Maybe we need to warn the Mexican DEA and see what bird falls from the nest," Agent Smalls suggested.

"No, neither of us can go. He's seen both of us before, especially you!"

"Shit!" Smalls exclaimed, looking Agent Davis in his eyes.

They had just listened to and recorded Real's entire conversation at their headquarters in Stuart.

"So, who do we send to watch him? Do we inform the Mexican DEA? FBI? Who?" Smalls asked. "Nobody?" she exclaimed, perplexed.

"Exactly, we will let him enjoy his vacation and wait until he returns to the States. Until then, we will bug all of his establishments, homes, and cars," Davis explained.

"I see why they say you're the best partner in the bureau," Smalls said with a smile on her face.

"How 'bout we go get us some coffee and breakfast at Denny's," Davis suggested.

"No donuts for a change!" Smalls added.

"No donuts, unless we flat on our way over there," Davis said, throwing a curveball that Smalls missed until a moment later.

"So, there is a spare, just in case?"

"Yep!" Davis replied with a smile on his face.

God, them eyes could never get too old. I can clearly see his past years of elegance, Agent Smalls thought as she led the way to the door with Davis on her heels.

She could feel his eyes trained on her nice, firm ass accentuated in her suit. When she stopped abruptly and turned around, she busted him staring at her ass.

"Is that your only concern?" Smalls asked impudently.

"Nah, it's part of my concerns," Davis retorted.

"Let's have breakfast at my hotel," Smalls suggested.

"Fine with me."

"I didn't think there would be any protest," she said with a girlish smile on her face as they proceeded out the front door of headquarters.

* * *

Polo proudly stepped out of the orphanage building on 129th in Overtown in Miami. He had just donated $20 million for the orphans across seas in Haiti and Africa. The ardent sun was too much for him to bear. Reaching into his coat pocket, he retrieved his Gucci shades.

"Hot day, Bo-Bo!" Polo spoke in Creole.

"Tell me about it," said Bo-Bo, who was armored and dressed in all back.

Walking toward the limousine, the chauffeur opened the door for his boss.

"Looks like everything went well, boss," the Haitian chauffeur spoke, seeing the smile on Polo's face.

"Yes indeed. It went well, Haitian," Polo responded as he stepped inside with Bo-Bo behind him.

"There's a Waffle House over on 169th. Let's go get us some breakfast," Polo demanded.

"Yes, sir, boss!"

As they moved through traffic, Polo's thoughts went to his young lion, Real. Since retreating from the drug business, Polo had seen Real make a tremendous amount of cash. He also had seen the newscast of the FBI killing one of his men, and he had the inside scoop. He was now just waiting on Real to inform him of the news. There was nothing in the data as of now about Real being in trouble. But Polo knew better than to expect that they weren't. Polo was stuck between a rock and facing a tough decision. He could re-enter the dope game to save his long-time plugs, or let the lion stand in the pit alone. As these thoughts spun around in his head while sitting at a red light at an intersection, when trouble pulled alongside him. On each side were three Haitian mafia men on Ninja 650s.

"Looks like we have company," Bo-Bo said, reaching for his AR-15 on the floor, only to be stopped short by Polo.

"What harm can they do to us?" Polo spoke in Creole.

Bo-Bo thought about what his boss was actually saying. When they looked at the men on the bikes, they had AK-47s in their hands, and they all squeezed together.

Chop! Chop! Chop! Chop! Chop!

Polo chuckled as the bullets ricocheted off the armored limousine. The men became furious and frustrated after seeing that their hit was a fiasco. Seeing that the bullets were useless, one of them quickly attached a bomb under the car.

"Go! Go! Go!" Bo-Bo yelled at the chauffeur, who was startled to death.

"Calm down, Bo-Bo, the gods are with us," Polo shouted as the limousine pulled off and the Ninja bikes dispersed from the area, going about their day.

Boom!

The bomb exploded, causing the limousine to elevate in the air about a foot off the ground. After the explosion, the limo continued down the road, unharmed by the bomb. The entire limousine was armored to ward off any type of threat. When Polo looked at Bo-Bo, he saw the sweat on his face and tossed him a towel.

"Trust the gods, Bo-Bo. They're the only ones more powerful than Mr. Polo," he said to a still-shaken Bo-Bo. "Black will never get that lucky, Bo-Bo. Remember, it's the gods to trust, not danger," Polo retorted.

* * *

"So, what did you think? Did you enjoy yourself?" Davis asked Smalls, who lay cozily cuddled up against his well-toned body while running her hands over his wonderful eight-pack abs.

"I think I underestimated you, Tod," Agent Smalls said.

"I knew you'd admit it. Don't let the gray hair fool you. Not every white man has White Man Syndrome."

"I can see that," Smalls said as she grabbed hold of his semi-erect dick and began stroking him back to life.

"Round two, and then we have round three in the shower," Smalls said as she sank below the covers and put Davis's dick in her mouth.

She slowly sucked his large dick while doing tricks with her mouth.

Damn! I can never get enough of you, black woman.

"That's right, bitch! Suck this dick!" Davis purred, talking dirty to Smalls like she liked it.

"Mmm," Smalls moaned as she sped up the pace of sucking his dick.

The sound of her slurping on his dick was music to his ears.

"Suck this dick, you pretty cunt!" Davis said as he grabbed her head and forced her to look into his eyes. "Yeah, look daddy in the eyes, baby!" he panted as he felt himself about to explode.

He stopped her and allowed her to stroke him off until he blew in her face.

"Ahh shit, woman! You got me!" he exhaled.

"No, we got each other," Smalls corrected.

* * *

Like everyone else, Bellda has seen the news and was worried about Real. She had tried to reach him a number of times, but to no avail.

"I can't believe he's acting like y'all just wasn't shit!" LeLe exclaimed while sitting at her table stirring her oatmeal.

"It's okay. He'll see how stupid his ass looks, sooner or later," Bellda retorted, placing her iPhone on the table and wiping the outburst of tears that came from so much built-up hurt.

"Come here, girl. You'll be alright!" LeLe rushed to her friend's side.

"I miss him so much!" Bellda cried as she broke down in LeLe's arms.

LeLe felt her friend's pain. Bellda was emotionally beaten and exhausted from worrying about when she would get to see Real again. She still loved him unconditionally and just wanted to be in the same room with him, even if they never talked.

"We goin' to get through this, Bellda. We have to!" LeLe said as she held Bellda in a consoling embrace and let her release all her pained tears.

"I need him!" she cried.

THIRTEEN

Cancun, Mexico

Real was enjoying himself, having a splendid time with his best friend, Kentucky, who lived in a luxurious beach house. Since Real had arrived, the two united brothers had been partying at different clubs every night. Kentucky had plastic surgery and was sporting a new look, and he also had a fiancée, Martha. Real became friendly with Martha's beautiful Mexican friend, Fatima.

"Damn, Kentucky, you're finally living how we planned," Real reminded him.

They were barbecuing out back of his beach house while Martha and Fatima prepared a salad and soft drinks for the kids. Martha had three kids from her previous relationship and was pregnant with a baby with Kentucky.

"We planned a master plan, and we are living the fruits of proper planning. Speaking of proper planning, brother," Kentucky began as he flipped over the ribs on the grill, "I think you need to really sit down and see how you gonna play these feds if they do come snooping."

"Shit! If they do come snooping, I guess we gonna run them off. That's why I'm asking for you to come back and be my eyes," Real said while sitting at the picnic table and taking a sip of his Budweiser.

"I want to come back and help you in whatever way, but what about Martha?" Kentucky inquired.

"Bring her."

"She has no green card."

"Neither do you. You still made it to Mexico," Real reminded him.

"True," Kentucky replied as he took a sip of beer. "So, what's the plan?"

"We tear down Delray until we find Big Chub. When we find him, we demand a ransom for him and then kill Black. I need a sharpshooter in position. You're the only man I know I can count on for that. I need you, brah!" Real explained.

Kentucky knew just like Real that it was a risk going back to the States, especially Martin County. Despite his adamant soul, he couldn't refuse the man who had helped him become a free man again. Kentucky was a sharpshooter who had dodged death row for a sniper conviction. A jury voted for him not to receive the sentence because the victims he chose to snipe were child molesters who had only served a small bid for their crimes. Instead of death, Kentucky received five life sentences without the possibility of parole. He was now a free and happy man, and his best friend needed him.

"I'm in! Give me two weeks behind you," Kentucky made up his mind.

"Thanks, brah," Real exclaimed, jumping from the picnic table and hugging Kentucky.

Neither Martha nor Fatima spoke any English, but they looked at the two friends and both smiled. However, they were unaware that their smiles would soon turn into disappointment.

* * *

Shamoney smiled when he walked through the visitation room door and saw his wife alone without the kids. When he made it to the table, Chantele stood up and then fell into his embrace. She kissed him long and passionately, like it was the last kiss on the face of the earth.

"You smell good, baby," Shamoney complimented his wife, who was showered in Rihanna's Rogue perfume.

"It's all for you, baby," Chantele said seductively.

"You ready for this?" Shamoney asked her.

"Shamoney, I've anticipated this day all week, baby."

"Oh yeah!" Shamoney retorted while licking his lips and rubbing his wife's thighs.

He slowly slid his hand under her jean skirt and felt the moist mound between her legs. When Shamoney looked over at Sgt. Thomas, she gave him a wink.

"Go to the restroom," Shamoney said to his wife.

"Now?"

"Yeah," he assured her. Shamoney nodded his head. When he noticed that she seemed nervous, he again told her that everything was okay.

"Don't worry, baby, everything's ten-four."

"Okay," Chantele said as she strutted off to the women's restroom.

Shamoney waited precisely two minutes before he made eye contact with Sgt. Thomas. He blew her a kiss, and she pouted her lips up furtively while blowing him one back. Shamoney then stood up and walked toward the restroom.

When Shamoney walked inside, there was no time to waste. Chantele tore away at his military belt, unzipped his uniform pants, and pulled out his erect dick. She stuck his dick in her mouth and put all that she could down her throat.

"Mmm!" she moaned.

She just wanted to taste him quickly.

Chanetele then sprung back up and leaned over the sink while simultaneously pulling up her skirt. Shamoney spread her ass cheeks apart and licked her asshole.

"Oh boy!" Chantele purred as his tongue licked her good.

He then quickly started sucking on her pussy lips and clitoris. When he was satisfied, he stood up and deeply entered his wife's tight pussy.

"Ahhh!" she purred loudly.

Shamoney covered her mouth and plunged deeply into her with powerful thrusts. Chantele's cries were muffled by his hand as he made love to his wife.

"Damn, this pussy good, baby. Shit!" Shamoney said as he and Chantele both came together to a strong electrifying orgasm.

Shamoney's knees went weak and he had to grab hold of the sink to keep from going down. "Damn!" he exclaimed as he let his seed drain inside of his wife.

"I love you, daddy," Chantele said while looking at her husband in the mirror.

"I love you too," Shamoney looked up and said.

* * *

Krystal smiled and blushed a bit when she saw her boyfriend, Juvie, pull up to her apartment complex. She finally listened to her homegirls about getting together with big money Juvie. Krystal was happy with him and felt special knowing that she was his number one—and the only one.

"Hey, baby!" Krystal said as she hugged Juvie when he stepped out of his conspicuous candy-apple-red Chevy Impala SS.

"What's good, ma?" Juvie retorted as he leaned in and kissed her slowly on her sexy lips.

Submissively, she parted her lips and let Juvie kiss her deeply.

"Mmm!" she let a moan escape.

Juvie grabbed Krystal's succulent ass in her black tights and instantly became erect.

"Y'all two could take all that smooching inside," Krystal's homegirl said after she stuck her head out of her apartment.

Krystal's friend's name was Shaye. She was a gorgeous five foot three, 120-pound redbone who was dating Juvie's brother, Capo.

"Bitch! Get some business and—!"

Boom! Boom! Boom! Boom!

The shots came out of the blue from a passing SUV. Two slugs pierced Juvie's back as he tried pushing Krystal out of the way. She hit the ground hard on her ass, falling in front of Juvie's Impala as the shots continued.

Shaye's and Krystal's screams were the last thing Juvie heard before his world went black.

"Nooo, Juvie!" Krystal screamed when she saw that Juvie was unresponsive.

A crowd quickly formed outside Krystal's apartment, and they felt terribly sorry for her because she was deeply in love with Juvie.

* * *

"I got that nigga, brah!" Krystal's ex-boyfriend, Marcus P., from Fort Pierce exclaimed.

He was an iron slanger. For months, he had been trailing Juvie, and had finally found the opportunity to nail him in the

101

presence of Krystal. With all the heat and beef between the Haitian mafia and Swamp Mafia, Marcus P. knew that he could get away as being a suspect. His homie, Demon, was the driver, and was praying that Chyna Man never caught wind of the hit that they had just carried out.

"I tried to hit that ho, too. The car saved her ass, brah!" Marcus P. exclaimed, crunked up from his adrenaline pumping rapidly throughout his body.

Man, yo' ass wasn't trying to hit that bitch. You'll be the first nigga in her face, Demon wanted to tell Marcus P., but he didn't want to rub him the wrong way.

When Demon looked up, he saw that they were being pulled over by a Martin County sheriff.

"Shit!" Demon exclaimed, hitting the steering wheel as he proceeded to pull over.

"What you doing, nigga? Hit it! We too dirty," Marcus P. shouted.

Both of them had guns, and the car was stolen.

"Let me handle—"

"Nigga, go or I'll pull!" Marcus P. snapped while pointing his .357 in Demon's face.

Demon, a killa himself, became furious and smashed on the gas pedal, causing Marcus P. to jerk back into his seat. The police immediately gave chase on I-95. Demon was an artistic driver, and Marcus P.'s confidence in him was high.

This nigga wants to put a gun in my face. I got this jealous-ass fuck nigga! Demon thought as he turned off an exit in Port St. Lucie.

The St. Lucie sheriffs joined the chase, trying to throw road spikes. Demon turned off into a neighborhood, slammed the stolen SUV into park, and hopped out without warning

Marcus P. Marcus P. then hopped out and initiated a shoot-out as he ran away from the police.

Boom! Boom! Boom!

Marcus P. never saw the man come out of his front door racking his shotgun and aiming it at Marcus's head.

Shlick-click, boom!

One shot to the chest, and Marcus. P dropped to the ground.

"Put down your weapon, sir!" a police officer screamed to the German man who just blasted away Marcus P.

"Okay, okay! He's on my property and tried to shoot me, officer," the German man said as he dropped his Perazzi MX2000 12-gauge shotgun and then put his hands up in the air.

"Don't worry, sir. We have it from here," an officer said to the man.

"You did what you had to do, sir, and what any good Samaritan would have done," a sergeant said as he looked down at a dead Marcus P. still holding a gun in his hand.

"Suspect lost. I repeat, second suspect lost. Lock down the area!" another sergeant shouted over the radio.

Demon was gone.

* * *

Juvie was grateful for the bulletproof vest that saved his life. When he awoke, the shrill of Krystal created a smile on his face.

Her cries had caused his perplexity to fade away. She cried while holding onto him, not seeing that his eyes were now open.

Damn! A nigga just tried to take me out! Juvie thought as he attempted to sit up but fell back into Krystal's arms from a sharp pain, which startled her to death.

"He's alive! Juvie, baby! Come back. Lord, he's alive!" Krystal shouted over the closing in of sirens that swarmed into the apartment complex.

"I'm fine," Juvie said, sitting up but wincing in pain.

Before the police could find out what was going on with the crowd of people, Juvie stormed inside Krystal's apartment with Shaye on their heels.

Juvie sat in the living room and slowly pulled off his black jacket and black T-shirt with the help of Krystal and Shaye.

"Your brother is on his way," Shaye informed.

"I'm okay." Juvie winced in pain when the woman removed his vest.

"Baby, they shot you in your damn back. Like, who does that?"

"Anybody that wants a nigga dead," Juvie said as he lay down on the sofa on his stomach.

"Shaye, girl, thank you so much," Krystal said as Capo walked into the apartment without knocking.

"Brah, you good?" Capo asked, worried about his brother.

Trap Money walked in after Capo and then locked the front door.

"Yeah, that shit knocked the wind out of my ass, that's all!"

"Man, we gotta find out who that was. I'm on straight go mode. Something tells me it's not them Haitians, brah," Capo said as he sat down in the chair while Trap Money took a seat on the love seat.

"I'm on go mode too, until we find out, brah!" Trap Money added.

"We gonna find out. Y'all know that I just need some rest right now. Baby, rub me down with that Icy Hot," Juvie commanded.

"Brah, hit us up when you get up. Stay inside, too. Crackas everywhere," Capo said as he stormed from the apartment with Shaye and Trap Money.

When everyone was gone, Krystal came back into the living room and rubbed some of the ointment on Juvie's sore back.

"Baby, promise me something," Krystal began.

"What's that, beautiful?"

"Promise me that you'll always keep that vest on."

"I will, baby. I'm always ten moves ahead of all them who want me out of the way," Juvie retorted while Krystal continued to apply the cream onto his back.

* * *

Johnny pulled over to the side of the road when he saw the unmarked SUV with its flashing red and blue lights. He was in Fort Pierce on 8th Street and Avenue D.

"What do y'all want now?" he said as Agents Smalls and Davis approached his truck.

"Mr. Johnny, tell me something, and I want you to be honest with me," Davis started.

"Do y'all have to pull me over for this?" Johnny asked.

He was glad that he wasn't in his hood, but he still worried about being seen talking to the police. He had a street cred that he needed to keep polished.

"We'll pull you over when we want to. Remember, you work for us. Your life in a cell feels like—"

"Man, what is it that y'all want?" he cut off Davis, growing more and more agitated.

"Two days ago a shooting occurred in Hobe Sound. No victim, but a suspicious SUV was stopped. Turns out it was stolen. One suspect was killed, but the other one got away. We've pulled prints from the SUV and got Demon Moye. Where will we find Demon?" Davis asked impudently.

Damn, Demon! Johnny thought.

Demon was one of his sergeants in the street. Johnny had heard how Marcus P. was killed and suspected of trying to kill Juvie. But there was no victim to compare the gun to the one found on Marcus P.

"Demon Moye!" Johnny pretended to search for recognition.

"Let's not play that game, Chyna Man, We know he's one of yours. We've got an address, but he's not there. So let's keep it business," Agent Smalls said.

Fuck, Demon! Johnny thought. "He's my sergeant. I could have him show up in the projects."

"Good, call us when you do," Davis said as he turned on his heels, with Smalls right behind him.

Damn, Demon! You stupid nigga! Johnny thought as he pulled off from the agitating FBI agents.

* * *

Despite wanting to remain in Delray to war it out with Real, Big Chub was having a much better time in Miami with Black than he had expected. His uncle had given him a trustworthy entourage of lethal killers, and Big Chub had been out every night increasing the murder rate in Miami by killing Zo'pound Haitians on every corner.

It wasn't easy, but Big Chub would prevail at every shoot-out and leave a Haitian flag bandana on the scene for ownership. It was 3:00 a.m. when Big Chub pulled up to a stash house owned by Polo's men. He had stumbled on the information after torturing his last kill. A Haitian named Bean quickly gave up Polo's traps in Miami before his death, thinking that he would live. The trap house in North Dade was occupied by a female who badly wanted to be a man. She was a dyke who fucked her bitches with strap-ons. Her name was Melissa, but she liked to be called Mel.

Big Chub was inside his SUV with three members of his six-man entourage: Haitian Rosco, Poppa, and King Zoe. All of them were from Haiti and smuggled in by Black years ago. When it came to murder, it was all they knew. Big Chub directed them every step of the way.

"Haitian King Zoe, go knock on the door and give us the green light."

"Okay, boss," King Zoe answered.

* * *

"Mmm!" a bad bitch named Keena moaned out as her girlfriend, Mel, fucked her from the back with a strap-on dildo and finger-fucked her asshole.

"You like this dick, huh?" Mel asked her girlfriend.

"Yes!" Keena exclaimed in ecstasy as she felt herself about to come.

"Come on his dick, baby!" Mel ordered as she sped up her pace and slapped Keena on her ass.

Smack!

"Yes, baby. I'm coming!" Keena shouted in pleasure as she convulsed to an orgasm.

They were in the living room when rapid knocks rapped on the front door.

Keena looked at Mel with a perplexed look. "You expecting someone?"

"No. We good. Shop's been closed, so that can't be no money, boo," Mel said.

"Go get in the shower. I'll be in there," Mel told Keena.

"Okay," Keena replied as she hurried to the bathroom while Mel got dressed in her black True Religion jeans and black T-shirt.

She grabbed her Glock .40 from underneath the sofa pillow, racked it, and slid it into her waistband.

Knock! Knock! Knock!

"I'm coming," Mel screamed as she walked to the front door.

When she got to the door and tiptoed to look out the peephole, she saw a Haitian man who she had never seen before. The only thing that made her consider there was no threat was the Zo'pound bandana around his neck. Had it been a Haitian flag, she would have started shooting. She was affiliated with Zo'pound and had straight hatred for the Haitian mafia.

Mel opened the door after unlocking it and stared the impish-looking Haitian in the eyes. "What's up? Who are you?"

Before Mel could get the words out, King Zoe grabbed her by her throat and throttled her to an unconscious state. When she was out, he let her body hit the floor. He then looked up at Big Chub in the SUV and gave him a thumb up.

When Big Chub came into the stash house, he walked toward the bathroom, where he heard the shower running. He tried the doorknob and stepped inside. The redolence of Irish

Spring strongly lingered. Behind the shower glass, Big Chub saw Keena showering while humming to a Beyoncé hit. Big Chub raised his AK-47 rifle, trained it on her, and then squeezed the trigger.

Chop! Chop! Chop! Chop! Chop!

The shower glass shattered as Keena's body was filled with a thirty-round clip.

Big Chub then inserted a fifty-round clip and walked into the living room. He saw that Mel was bound naked with her hands behind her back on the floor.

"Grab her legs and pull them apart," Big Chub told Poppa and Haitian Rosco, who quickly did as they were ordered.

When Big Chub looked down at Mel's nicely-trimmed phat pussy, his dick became hard. But instead of putting his dick inside, his desire was to shove his AK-47 in instead. When he did, Mel moaned out in pain, unable to scream from the duct tape over her mouth.

"Remove the tape, Poppa," Big Chub demanded.

When Poppa did as instructed, Mel begged and panted for her life to be spared. "Please!"

"I'ma ask you two questions, and I want the truth. Do you hear me?" Big Chub asked.

"Yes, I hear you."

"Who do you work for under Polo?" he asked.

"Snake! I work for Snake," Mel answered in pain.

"Where can I find him?"

"I don't know. He always comes to me. I really don't—"

Chop! Chop! Chop!

Before Mel could finish, Big Chub squeezed the trigger and sent AK-47 slugs into her bloody pussy. He then pulled out and emptied the clip into her body, leaving her bullet-riddled. He then tossed a Haitian flag over her body. The entourage inconspicuously left the scene and headed back to Miami Gardens.

FOURTEEN

Three Weeks Later

Tick Tock!

The club again was packed beyond capacity. Everyone was there to see Lil Boosie live in concert. Security was jam-packed to keep peace among the club. Kentucky and Chucky were having the thrill of their lives. Their plastic surgeries paid off well, as no one would be able to recognize them. Swamp Mafia was in the VIP section enjoying watching the exotic dancers and strippers.

"Man, you really put this shit together!" Kentucky exclaimed over the loud music serenading the club.

"Yeah, don't forget, we made this happen, brah," Real said as he racked the pool balls for a round with Chucky.

"Kentucky, watch how I take Real's ass to retirement," Chucky exclaimed.

"Damn, brah! Chucky talking like he superb on this shit!" V-Money said to Real.

"Well," Real said, pulling out a fat wad of cash and slamming it down on the table. "I like me, against all odds."

"I like Real, Chucky, for $1,200," V-Money bet.

"I call that," Chucky replied.

"I like me for $1,200 too!" Real added while chalking the tip of his pool stick.

"I call that too," Chucky confidently replied.

* * *

The Latino man and the white man with the gold in his mouth were two new additions to the Swamp Mafia. Agents Smalls and Davis were at a dead-end trying to find out anything about them in the FBI database. Johnny was at a loss as to whom they were as well, and no amount of pressure could frighten Johnny. He simply didn't know who they were.

"I'ma see how close I can get to the white guy, Davis," Smalls said.

"So you really do have a thing for white boys, huh?" Davis retorted, with a hint of insecurity in his voice.

They were sitting in a television van watching the surveillance monitor of the inside of the club, which they had successfully bugged.

"Come here!" Smalls demanded as Davis seemed to be in his own feelings about Smalls's prospect of dealing with another man—an attractive man.

"What?" Davis nonchalantly asked.

"Don't even act like that," Smalls purred as she slid over to him and climbed into his lap, straddling him in the rolling chair.

"Listen, old man!"

"Old man, huh?"

"Yeah, old man. There's no need to get upbeat 'bout nothing. We're a team, and there's no turncloak in me, mister," Smalls said as she kissed Davis on the lips.

As the kiss intensified, Davis caressed her ass, removed her holster, and unbuckled her gray slacks. She slid out of her pants and then pulled down Davis's zipper. She stuck his erect dick into her mouth and sucked him slowly. Satisfied with his erection, she straddled him again and slowly descended onto it.

"Yes, baby," Smalls purred as she began to rapidly ride Davis's dick. She filled her pussy with his cock and rode it like he was a wild bull.

Smack!

Davis slapped Smalls on the ass and then pulled up her shirt in an attempt to caress her caramel breasts. But he became disappointed when he saw that she had on a vest.

Shit! he thought, badly wanting to taste her nipples.

The thought alone made him explode inside her, which made her come on cue herself.

"Uhh! Shit!" Smalls moaned.

"Look!" Davis said, pointing at the surveillance monitor showing the club.

* * *

Something was wrong with Johnny, and Real knew better than anyone else in the club when his brother was bothered.

"Johnny, take a walk with me," Real whispered in his ear as they walked out of the VIP area.

When Real and Johnny were inside Real's office, Real turned around, grabbed Johnny by his shoulders, and looked him in his eyes.

"What's wrong, little brother? And please don't tell me nothing!"

"Brah, I'm okay. Just trying to hold this shit together," Johnny said.

Truth be told, Johnny was feeling so lowly of himself for going out like a busta. He couldn't believe how he had capitulated so easily to the FBI. Every moment he was setting up his brother was just killing him inside.

"Johnny, I'm more than your friend."

"I know, my brother."

"If you got a lot of shit on your mind, then you could rest on going to Georgia."

"When you need me to go to Georgia? I thought we were still in a drought," Johnny exclaimed.

"I'm breaking the drought tonight, and I'ma need you to hit the road in two days. The medical examiner isn't releasing Su'Rabbit's body until sometime next month, so I need you to make his plans too," Real said.

"I'ma need you to help me with the funeral arrangements. I'm not equipped to make them myself," Johnny admitted.

"Don't worry, brah. I'm with you all the way. I just need you to focus. We got money to continue stacking," Real retorted.

"Okay, brah. I got you," Johnny replied.

"Where's Courtney?" Real asked.

"She's okay. We just fuck friends. Shit, she'd slide with the both of us if the money was right," Johnny said with an impish smirk on his face, knowing that Smalls was somewhere listening.

"I'll pass, brah! I already got too many partners," Real said.

* * *

When Johnny came out of his brother's office and entered the VIP area, he was shocked to see Agent Smalls dressed in her "Courtney" outfit dancing with Real's homeboy that Johnny knew as Dirt.

"What the fuck! This bitch don't waste no time!" he mumbled to himself as he watched Kentucky get his feel on with Courtney.

When Smalls saw the look on Johnny's face, she gave him a wink and blew him a kiss.

"Fuck you, pig!" Johnny mouthed off to her.

Smalls read his lips and smiled brightly as Johnny left the room.

"So, you're from Philly, huh?"

"South Philly. Let's be specific."

"Courtney Queen. Pretty name. Are you related to—?"

"No!" Smalls replied. "I just told you I'm from Philly. I'm on business. All I do is dance."

"That's all?" Kentucky asked.

"Well, I drink too. And speaking of drink, could you buy me a bottle of Peach Cîroc? I'll show you a trick," Smalls seductively whispered in his ear.

Kentucky looked around and saw everybody from Swamp Mafia in their own world. As badly as he didn't want to miss Boosie's set, as Boosie was running late, he was ready to see Courtney's trick behind closed doors.

"How 'bout we take this party to our own private VIP section? Just me and you?"

"Your money must be long, and you must see the diamond in your eyes," Smalls retorted seductively.

"My boy owns this joint, and I see more than a diamond. I see a precious ruby. I'm not pressing for a one-night stand. I'm having a good time with a beautiful woman," Kentucky said to Smalls.

I gotta get this bitch. She's gorgeous as hell! Kentucky thought while caressing her ass.

"Okay. I'll go private with you!" Smalls told him after giving it a moment of feigned contemplation.

"Let's get out of here!" Kentucky said as he walked out of VIP with Courtney and down the adjunct hallway, where there was another private VIP section in a sound-proof room.

When they neared the private VIP area, Smalls was hit with a revelation: *We didn't bug the private rooms. Shit!* she thought.

"Are you okay?" Kentucky asked her, since she had a nervous look on her face.

She simply looked at him and smiled. "I'm okay. I'm just a little nervous that we're going private. I don't normally do this," Smalls explained.

"We could abort and go back if you want."

"I'm okay. We're here now. Let's continue to have fun," Courtney continued.

Kentucky shook his head up and down. He paid the six four, 250-pound bouncer $1,200 to book a private room. Kentucky was feeling like the man in the place after beating his conscience of indecisiveness about taking Courtney to VIP.

She seems different from everyone else dancing in the club, he thought.

Inside the glowing-red, luxurious room, Kentucky sat on the red leather French seat and allowed Courtney to give him a lap dance. Fighting the temptation and losing, he pulled out his dick and stroked himself while caressing her succulent ass as she danced to the R. Kelly hit "Down Low." When Smalls turned around and saw Kentucky masturbating, she was shocked, but she bridled her emotion. He stared her in the eyes as he continued to slowly stroke himself.

"Show me that trick you promised me," Kentucky said, biting his bottom lip and revealing his top gold grill.

"First, take a drink," Smalls said as she passed him the bottle of Cîroc.

Kentucky grabbed the bottle and took a long swig. Once satisfied, Smalls turned around and started dancing to the Drake hit "I Need a Dance" blaring from the speakers

She looked back and saw Kentucky stroking fast. She made her ass cheeks clap together while looking back into Kentucky's eyes.

"For you, Dirty!" Smalls said as she bent over to touch her toes.

She pulled her boy shorts up to show Kentucky her phat pussy, and that's when he exploded all over her ass.

"Damn, man! We definitely gotta kick it!" Kentucky said, panting out of breath.

"That's fine with me. Let's just take it slow, okay?" Smalls said.

"Okay, baby. Let me clean up, and then we can just chill," he said as he stood up and walked into a restroom around the corner in the room.

When she heard the door close, she raised the Cîroc bottle to the light and smiled when she saw his sweaty palm prints on the bottle.

"Thanks, Dirt!" she said as she stormed from the room to get as far away from him as possible.

When Kentucky walked out of the restroom and saw that his date was gone, he shook his head.

I knew she was afraid. I shouldn't have done that, Kentucky thought. *Paying for that room was a waste of money.*

"It's okay, I'll just find me a bitch I know about her money," Kentucky said out loud as he walked out of the private room.

When he made it back into the club's VIP section, everyone was still having a good time. When he looked around, he saw Johnny and V-Money shooting pool. There was a crowd around the table, and it was evident to Kentucky that they were gambling again.

Shit, I just lost $1,200. I'm gonna try to get my money back, he thought as he neared the pool table.

Real and Chucky were up next. It was a fifty-fifty bet when it came to Real and Chucky, because the bet could go any way.

I'm going to put my money on Chucky and then side bet on Real, Kentucky thought.

* * *

Once back inside the television van, she handed the Cîroc bottle to Agent Davis, with a smile on her face.

"Looks like you just had the time of your life," he said.

"Shut up! Please tell me how we forgot to bug the private rooms?" Smalls asked Davis.

"I thought we only needed the office, dance floor, and VIP area. I never thought about the possibility of you going private. Don't worry yourself. You made a good decision, baby," Davis said as he pulled off in the van heading to their headquarters in Martin County. "Something tells me that we could break Mr. Dirt like Johnny," Davis said.

"Don't count on it. He's too gangsta!" Smalls added.

* * *

When Snake and his goon, Money Lane, pulled up to the light on their Ninja 650s, he saw that the next intersection was busy with cars leaving Club 54 onto Broward Boulevard.

"Get ready, Lane," Snake said to his goon, who was a sharpshooter and the perfect partner to bring to a shoot-out. Snake retrieved his MAC-10 from his backpack while Money Lane grabbed his AR-15 rifle. It was nearing 3:00 a.m., and only a couple Broward County police were out.

When the light turned green, both Snake and Money Lane burned rubber on their Ninjas and raced toward the next intersection. Half the distance to the club, they stood up together and aimed at the crowd of Haitian mafia men pimping in the parking lot next to a candy-red Impala. Together they initiated a deadly fusillade.

Tat! Tat! Tat! Tat! Tat!

The Haitian mafia were taken off guard and hit by the men driving sixty miles per hour and dropped to their deaths. The Broward police tried to return fire, but they missed the artistic drivers. Snake and Money Lane both made abrupt U-turns and came back toward the club, one behind the other driving on the median. Snake took down two police officers and more Haitian mafia members while Money Lane took out three more police officers who tried to scramble to safety. Snake and Money Lane then dispersed at the intersection and went their separate ways, leaving Club 54 a bloody sight.

* * *

Juvie, Capo, and Trap Money pulled up to 8th Street in Delray and jumped out of a stolen pickup truck. They initiated deadly gunfire on slipping Haitian mafia members who were outside a trap house. A couple of them were taken quickly, while some had a chance to stand their ground. But just like fallen soldiers, they failed too.

"Come here, stupid-ass Haitian," Juvie shouted as he grabbed one of them by his dreadlocks and squeezed the trigger of his Mini-14, exploding the head of the Zoe.

Capo and Trap Money both entered the trap house and killed everyone in sight. Inside a back room, Capo found three nude women who were cooking and bagging up the cocaine for the Haitians.

Chop! Chop! Chop! Chop!

Capo killed all three of the workers and then left the trap with his 4-Life crew.

Every night, the 4-Life crew members put in work for Swamp Mafia. They were family and were rocking with Real 100 percent. Real's beef was theirs, and their beef was Real's. Swamp Mafia was what kept them living a lavish lifestyle, and they were indebted to their Swamp Mafia cousins.

"Let's hit up Killa County, so I can go handle this shit!" Juvie said to Trap Money, who was driving the stolen truck.

Trap Money pulled into a community park in Fort Pierce City on 29th Street an hour and thirty minutes later.

"Y'all wait here. I'll be back," Juvie said.

"You sure you don't want me to come with you, brah?" Capo asked Juvie.

"Nah, lil brah. I got this one. Just keep the truck hot," Juvie said as he hopped down from the truck and then walked through a small pathway that led him over to the next street.

When Juvie made it to the target house, he unscrewed the light bulb with gloved hands and then rapped on the front door of the project apartment. He heard footsteps and then the door being unlocked.

Boom! Boom! Boom! Boom! Boom!

"Now you can join your pussy-ass son!" Juvie said as he ran off back into the night.

Juvie put two and two together after finding out the news about Marcus P's. run-in with Martin County sheriffs. He was acting off instinct and now was waiting for Demon Moye to slip up. Killing Marcus P.'s mother made him feel good. There was no way Juvie was about to let a dead man get away with trying to take him out.

FIFTEEN

Agent Chad Sullivan couldn't thank Agents Davis and Smalls enough for breaking the investigation on the escapes from Martin County Correctional Institute. Sullivan was the leading agent in the case, and now he had his escapees in the scope. However, disappointment would soon take over.

"This is wonderful news, boss," Sullivan said to Director Tom Johnson while sitting at a conference table in a conference room.

Also present were Agents Davis and Smalls, and Sullivan's partner, Swells, who was a thirty-year veteran with Sullivan. Johnson stood from his seat at the end of the table, after hearing that a positive read came back from the FBI on the fingerprints that Smalls had gotten from Dirt. Johnson called for an emergency meeting.

"For the prints to come back as an escapee's, and for this escapee, Jacob Spears, to be affiliated with Jermaine 'Real' Wilkins, there's more to the picture. Can anybody answer that?" Director Johnson asked while scrolling down on his laptop on which no one could see the screen.

Agent Davis knew Johnson too well. He knew that Johnson already had a theory, and like every time when he voiced his theory, it was proven to be true. Johnson was now seeing where his agents were at in their heads.

"Sullivan, this is your case. Can you tell me what's behind this picture? We have escapees. Of course, that was your job, right? But you didn't break the case. You made a mistake somewhere, and it was a big one," Johnson explained to Sullivan, who looked at Swells for answers that Swells could not give him.

"I'm at a loss, sir," Sullivan admitted.

"Good ownership. Davis, if this was your case from the beginning, instead of assisting Agents Sullivan and Swells, what immediate grounds would you have covered?" Johnson asked Davis, who had opened a folder and began to read from a document he had prepared for the meeting.

"Sir, coming into this investigation months ago, I was briefed by Agent Swells that Agent Sullivan was the lead agent. I only assisted in the K-9 unit until I was called by locals of Martin County about information pertinent to my own lead case. Me and my partner, Stanley, both left the K-9 unit and went to act on our own case. To answer your question, had I been the lead agent on the escapees, I would have first found out about Jacob's past cellmates," Davis said as he pulled out a paper from his folder and slid it over to Johnson.

"When me and my partner, Agent Smalls, did that ourselves, sir, we found an interesting link. Jacob (Dirt/Kentucky) Spears was once cellmates with Jermaine (Real) Wilkins."

Shit! Sullivan thought, not believing how he had let that slide by him.

"And frankly, I'll say that it's Agents Sullivan and Swells's mistake, which is crucial."

"Jackass!" Swells exploded, not appreciating how Davis was trying to steal their case.

"It's our credit, sir, and I believe that if we keep Jacob under the scope, we could bring him down along with Real, Black, and his buddy Chucky. Are we sure it's Chucky? Yeah, because Mr. Juan Hernandez is still living with the scar behind his ear," Davis explained.

"Well, I can agree with everything. My question to you, Mr. Davis, is that if we continue to keep the escapees under the scope, will we be making a mistake by not taking them down now?" Johnson asked.

It was something that Agent Davis had to think about quickly and come up with his most confident answer.

If we take them down, Real again will be prompted to fall back until he feels that it is safe, Davis thought.

Davis looked over at Smalls, who winked at him, before he sighed and then spoke. "No, sir. We will not be making a mistake by not taking them down now."

"Okay, then we will let them hang out. Agent Sullivan, I'm keeping you on this case but reassigning you. Agent Davis will now be the lead agent, so what he says goes!" Director Johnson instructed. He then closed his laptop and departed from the room.

"Thanks, boss. You ruined my day," Sullivan said as he walked out of the room.

"Good job, Davis," Smalls sincerely said.

"Yeah, good job, pal. I see you still have the fire in you," Swells sarcastically complemented Davis.

"I'll never go dull," Davis said.

"I can vouch for that!" Smalls added, unaware that Swells hadn't missed the understatement like she had intended.

After leaving headquarters with another burden to bare and load to carry, Davis and Smalls retired for the afternoon at Davis's hotel in Port St. Lucie. They made congratulatory love and celebrated over pizza and champagne. Their happiness was genuine and so loud that neither of them heard the clock ticking.

Tick! Tock!

* * *

Real had just hopped out of the shower when his phone rang. He walked over to the nightstand and answered. "Hello?"

"This is a collect call from Shamoney. To accept this call at the Centry Correctional Institution, please press 1," the automated voice said.

Beep!

Real pressed 1, not needing to listen to any further prompts.

"This call is subject to monitoring and recording. Thank you for using GTL," the automated voice said, clearing the way for Real and Shamoney to converse.

"What's up, my nigga?" Real was exhilarated, since he was glad to hear Shamoney's voice.

"Shit! You tell me, brah? I'm ready to see you," Shamoney said.

"I know you are. A nigga just been running around. Is you getting all the money?" Real asked.

"I get everything you send to Chantele. That last pound had everyone going crazy, feel me?"

"Hell yeah. Shit! I just gave her some more. Anything you need me to do for you?" Real asked.

"Yeah, man. Gina's still going to court, and I need her to get a mouthpiece."

"Say no more, brah. I'll talk to Mr. Wells and have him find me the best," Real answered.

"I heard 'bout Su'Rabbit and Juvie. How's Chyna Man taking everything?" Shamoney asked, concerned for his baby brother.

"He trying his best, brah," Real said as he sat on his bed and was hit with a retrospection of he and Bellda making love.

"He's keepin' his head on his shoulders. Su'Rabbit was that nigga's round and brother," Shamoney said.

"You have sixty seconds remaining," the automated voice said.

"Brah, about Bellda. She wrote me. Trying to work it out," Shamoney said.

"Thank you for using GTL," the automated voice chimed in before disconnecting the call.

It didn't take a rocket scientist to figure out what Real was about to say out of his mouth: "Sorry, lil brah, but Bellda is dead to me. I give a bitch only one time to cut me," Real exclaimed as he lay back on his bed, just on cue with the phone ringing again.

When he looked at the caller ID, a smirk swept across his face.

Yeah, I need that chocolate shit right about now, Real thought.

"Hello," Real answered.

"What's up, boo? I see you're back in town. Is there any way we can get together? It's been a while," Mookie seductively said to Real.

"Hell yeah! Where you at?" Real asked.

"I'm five minutes away."

"I'm here. Just walk in and come upstairs with nothing on," Real demanded.

"Okay," Mookie agreed, letting loose a girlish giggle before she hung up.

Damn! That bitch know she got some good-ass pussy, Real thought as he closed his eyes.

Like Real had demanded, Mookie came into the room five minutes later with nothing on. She woke up Real, who had dozed off, by planting kisses down his body. When she made it to his erect dick, Mookie climbed in bed and positioned herself in a sixty-nine position. Real began licking her ass while he finger-fucked her phat pussy.

Smack!

Real slapped her ass and then softly bit her ass cheek.

"Who's pussy is this?" Real asked a moaning Mookie.

"It's yours, daddy!" Mookie purred as she slid up to Real's dick.

She reached behind her and slowly descended on his cock reverse cowgirl style. Mookie wildly rode his dick and took all of him in her phat pussy. When she came, they came together.

"Umm! Shit!" Mookie exhaled in pleasure. "Baby, this pussy been waitin' for you to return. Now I want you to beat this pussy up like it was the last pussy on earth," Mookie ordered Real, and he did exactly what she had asked.

They fucked all night and got drunk on Remy Martin until the sun came up. Mookie had really done a number on Real, and he wanted more of her—every day now. She was officially his bitch on the down low, until he handled his beef with Black. He didn't want to deal with how Lala would take it when she found out that he was fucking one of her Ms. Gorgeouses.

* * *

Juvie and Capo heard Coy's tow truck coming down the road before he pulled up. When they stopped outside, Coy was backing the truck into their yard, and T-Gutta had pulled up in his .745 with Lunatic trailing him.

T-Gutta pulled his car around back and stepped out to greet Juvie and Capo. "What's up, my niggas?"

"Three hos, one me," Juvie said, giving T-Gutta and Lunatic a dap.

"Three hos on me," Capo said, dapping the two men.

"Okay, let's get this shit started, my nigga," T-Gutta said as he walked back to his .745 to retrieved the kilos from the stash spots under the driver and passenger seats.

On the back of Coy's tow truck bed were five Toyotas with stash spots in their trunks. Today was a big shipment. Each of the cars held fifty kilos of cocaine, and there were going to be five drops in Tampa, St. Pete, Orlando, Ocala, and Tallahassee. The following week, Real and T-Gutta would be sending Coy to drop off another load out of state along the East Coast in South Carolina, Virginia, Delaware, New York, and New Jersey. As T-Gutta and Lunatic loaded up the cars, the DEA was controlling the see-through drone that no one had noticed.

* * *

"So, now we know that Travon Jamison is second-in-command of the streets," Davis said to Johnny, who was sitting in the backseat of the unmarked car while Smalls went inside the Hess gas station to grab a snack for them.

"Yeah, that's T-Gutta. He's second-in-command of the streets," Johnny informed Agent Davis.

"So tell me something," Davis began, looking at Johnny in his rearview mirror. "Your brother chooses one of his friends to be second-in-command instead of his brother. Shamoney's in prison. Wouldn't you think that torch would be passed to you?" Davis asked curiously.

"I think anybody would think like that, but apparently, it's not my call."

Unless I knock off T-Gutta and become his replacement, Johnny thought.

"Well, partner, I just find that kind of odd. Maybe the brotherly love isn't in his heart for you," Davis said as an understatement.

Johnny's silence let Davis know that his words had hit home. A second later, Smalls came out of the Hess station and handed Davis a bag of blue cheese buffalo chips and a Coke.

"Thanks," he said, opening the bag and offering Smalls a chip.

"No thanks," Smalls retorted as Davis pulled off.

"Johnny?" Smalls called on Johnny.

"What, pig?" Johnny said.

"Excuse me, but what makes you less of a pig than me?" Smalls asked him. Johnny wouldn't immediately reply.

"She's right," Davis added. "Just like I'm right about your brother not loving you as a brother," Davis said as he pulled into an abandoned lot.

Davis put the unmarked car in park and then turned around in his seat to look at Johnny.

"Tomorrow, do your routine route and then come back on time. We're watching you every step of the way. If you try to run, when we catch your ass, in the box you go. We have enough to bring everybody down, including you. So, it's either you're gonna be the one to come out of this situation with no scars or you will fall like everyone else. You make the decision of your own fate," Davis explained.

"Man! You ain't gotta worry about me. I told you that from the beginning. Since day one, I've been cooperative, man. When will y'all start looking out for me?" Johnny asked.

"And what is it that you want from us?" Smalls asked.

"Right now, I feel like a sore thumb. I need y'all to pick up someone other than me. If you don't, shit's gonna look too obvious when y'all do hit," Johnny exclaimed.

"We got you," Smalls sincerely said, never looking at Davis.

She could feel Davis's eyes burning a hole in her face. But Johnny was right. She even thought about it herself. Someone else needed to be picked up from the Swamp Mafia. Until Davis brought news to the DEA that he had found someone to bring down Real, the DEA had been arresting anyone who looked like a pusher and interrogating them, but getting no one to give up Real, the kingpin of the Treasure Coast. If Davis didn't understand, Smalls would enlighten him later.

But now Smalls had made the final decision to arrest someone else soon. *But who?* she wondered.

* * *

"He's gonna be upset, Real. I know he is," Chantele said to Real, who sat at her kitchen table eating her delicious soul food.

"You did what you thought was best for her, Chantele, and I agreed too."

They had just watched Gina be carried out on a gurney and transported to a mental hospital in Port St. Lucie. Gina's demented state being treated by Ms. Addie alone was no longer working for Gina. Real had stopped by to support Chantele through her self-conscious grief. She knew that Shamoney wanted the best for Gina so she could bounce back for the sake of her kids. Just like he wouldn't deny Shada Jr., he also would not leave Gina for dead.

Chantele was at the kitchen sink washing and drying dishes while Real ate like a hog. When he looked closer at her, he noticed that she was putting on a bit of weight.

Damn! She's either fucking on lil brah or eatin' too much chicken and bread, Real thought.

When Chantele heard the twins crying, she hurried to the living room. Real stood and walked with her to help assist. When they entered the living room, Real picked up Shada Jr., who was trying to stand with the help of the sofa. Real found it amusing, and it warmed his heart.

"Hey there, lil man. What you doing?" Real asked as he tossed Shada Jr. up and down in the air, causing him to laugh.

Chantele grabbed both girls and sat on the couch. She whipped out her breasts and fed both of her daughters. When Real looked back at her, he saw her still-firm breasts and felt uncomfortable. Chantele sensed his discomfort and smiled.

"It's okay, Real. It's natural. Think of the people in Haiti, Africa, and other poor lands where they walk around topless," Chantele said.

"Yeah, I guess," Real said as he sat down on the sofa next to her.

"So, where is all this new weight coming from? You slimmed down after you had the girls," Real asked impudently.

Chantele broke out in laughter while trying her best not to piss herself.

"What's so funny?" he asked.

"Maybe you need to ask your brother why he's makin' babies in prison," Chantele responded.

"Damn! So, brah got it like that, huh?" Real retorted.

"Yep, and it was a fun experience," Chantele answered before she gave him the whole story of how she and Shamoney had made their third addition to the family.

"Four kids and still a young nigga!" Real said, shaking his head.

"Real, can I ask you a question?"

"Yeah, what's up?"

"If I was to tell you that Bellda still loves you and that she never meant to hurt you, would you consider giving her at least a chance to explain herself and see where things go from there?" Chantele asked Real.

"Chantele, I know that's your girl and all, but she fucked up!" Real said as he stood up with Shada Jr. He placed him down on the sofa, grabbed his jacket from the coat rack, and then looked back at Chantele. "A woman only has one chance to burn me, and she did that, Chantele. I felt like I was sleeping with the enemy," Real said as he walked out the front door.

He was tired of everyone trying to put him and Bellda back together. His mind was made up. Bellda was dead to him.

SIXTEEN

"**Y**o, Crazy, we need some more product on 9th and some more eyes. Them downtown niggas been spinning bins all night," Tankhead said to Crazy Zoe.

Tankhead was a lieutenant who informed Crazy Zoe of the latest drive-by shootings between their enemies. He was also a pusher and lethal Haitian for the Haitian mafia under Crazy Zoe. He was standing outside Crazy Zoe's conspicuous Range Rover when he saw the nimble movement out of the corner of his eye. When he looked, he barely got a scream out when the man hanging out the window squeezed off shots from his AK-47.

Chop! Chop! Chop! Chop!

"Oh shit!" Crazy Zoe screamed while immersing in his front seat and grabbing his MAC-11.

His back window shattered, and he could tell that the shooters were coming at him next. Taking his chances, he peeped over his backseat at the same time his back tires abruptly went flat.

Shit! Crazy Zoe thought as he saw the assassins coming his way.

* * *

Juvie and Capo were dropping everyone in sight on 8th Street in Delray.

The nigga in the candy-coated Range Rover is trapped, as is anybody inside with him, Juvie thought.

"Go on the other side!" Juvie told Capo, who began creeping and sending rapid slugs from his AK-47 at the rear and left side of the Range Rover.

Trap Money stayed in the stolen Dodge Durango blocking off the street. As Capo continued to squeeze off shots along with Juvie, Crazy Zoe surprised them, leaping from the Range Rover on foot and squeezing off his MAC-11.

Tat! Tat! Tat! Tat!

Juvie was taken by surprise and hit in his chest. Twice within months, he was fortunate to be wearing a vest.

Crazy Zoe quickly ran through a yard across the street. The impact from the slugs dropped Juvie to his knees. When Capo made it to the other side of the Range Rover, he saw that it was useless to pursue Crazy Zoe.

His brother, Juvie, was in pain, holding on to consciousness. It was time to go. Capo looked down at a dead Tankhead and squeezed twice and hit him in the face before he rushed over to his brother's side.

When Capo made it to Juvie, Trap Money was already up on them. Capo helped Juvie to his feet and then placed him in the backseat of the Durango. Trap Money then quickly drove them off the scene.

"That's the Zoe who killed Kenny and J-Mack." Juvie winced in pain while hunched over. "My shoulder's number, brah!" Juvie exclaimed as he began to feel a burning pain.

"Man, let me check you out," Capo said as he pulled his brother by his shoulder.

"Aww shit!" Juvie exclaimed in severe pain.

When Capo saw the wet spot on Juvie's black T-shirt, he knew that his brother was hit.

It was dawning on Juvie that the pain he was feeling was an actual gunshot wound, but before he could tell Capo, he passed out.

"Get us to the hospital!" Capo screamed to Trap Money, who increased his speed.

* * *

Big Chub was back in Delray Beach and was listening to a frustrated Crazy Zoe vent about his escape from death.

"Them niggas was coming at me, Haitian," Crazy Zoe exclaimed as he paced the den floor while Boxhead and Chub looked at him. "All I seen is Tankhead go down, and then them niggas let off fifty more! Shit! I want them niggas!"

"Man, don't let your frustration cause you to wreck out, Haitian. We know exactly how we gonna play this. I got good news to tell y'all both," Big Chub said as he stood up and looked at a curious Boxhead and Crazy Zoe.

"What is that, Haitian?" Crazy Zoe asked Big Chub.

"We got Shamoney. It's a done deal," Big Chub retorted.

"Real soon the Swamp Mafia about to be mourning, and that's when we light their day up, Haitian. It's called a death trap," Big Chub explained.

Damn right, it is good news! Crazy Zoe thought.

"At the same time, we don't know how the aftermath may come," Big Chub added.

Fuck the aftermath! I'm bringing the party to these niggas every day! Crazy Zoe thought. "I'm still about to make these niggas drop like flies. They tried to take me out by myself."

"Don't worry, brah. We gonna handle up," Boxhead told his brother.

* * *

When Robert (Rob Bass) Wilkins stepped into the crowded visitation room, he looked around for his visitors. The redolence of popcorn strongly lingered. He smiled when he saw his ex-wife, Michele, and his daughter, Precious. He first hugged Michele and then gave both of them kisses on their foreheads.

"Surprise visit, huh?" Rob Bass said as he took his seat at the long table, opposite the women.

"I told you the closer you get to coming home, the more we will see you," Michele spoke.

Despite their divorce, Michele and Rob Bass still remained friends.

"Daddy, you're getting too big now!" Precious exclaimed, looking at the huge size of his arms.

"Years of lifting weights," he replied. "So, with me being in Miami now, I'll see more of you, but will I see anyone else?"

"I can't speak for your sons. Their focus is on the streets. I can only speak for me and your daughter," Michele explained.

"Real did want me to ask you if you are getting all the money he sends you?" Precious inquired.

"Yeah, tell Real—"

"What I tell you 'bout calling your son Real? It's Jermaine, last time I remember naming him, and you were there!" Michele explained.

"Michele, it's the boy's nickname. We can't take that from no grown man," Rob retorted.

"Whatever," Michele said as she rolled her eyes at him as he began to chuckle.

"Baby, go order us something to eat. Here, use my card," Rob said to Precious as he handed her his ID/bank card.

"Why is it so heavy, daddy?" she joked.

"Because it's bands on top of bands," Rob answered.

As he watched his daughter—and only daughter—go stand in line, he took in how much she had developed since the last time he had seen her when he was incarcerated at Atlanta Federal Penitentiary. She was eleven then; now she was fifteen—almost sixteen.

"She's definitely growing fast, baby."

"So now I'm 'baby.' What did I tell you, Robert?"

Damn! This woman has changed too much for me, Rob thought. "Michele, do you remember before I got busted what I told you?"

"I remember everything, Robert," Michele retorted, and then tried her best to bridle her emotions.

Despite giving her life to Christ, she still loved her ex-husband. It was easy to move on from a man who wasn't there physically, but mentally was another token. She felt she needed strength to move on from a man she had been with from the beginning of Adam and Eve.

"You told me that you were planning on leaving the game, and if they somehow got you before, to always be around for you," Michele said while wiping her eyes.

"That's all I ask of you. When I see my son, I'ma let him know that I want him to leave the game alone before it's too late. To lose any of my kids to death or the system would destroy me, Michele."

"We're not going to lose them. Come, let's pray together," Michele said as she grabbed his hand and began praying.

* * *

Real wasn't a happy camper when he discovered that Juvie had been shot in his shoulder. He was sending out Juvie with his 4-Life circle every night dropping Haitians in Delray. Somebody knew where to find Big Chub, and he was desperately trying to nail him. After meeting up with Polo, Real met with T-Gutta at his luxurious home in Port St. Lucie that he shared with LeLe.

"So what's up with Shamoney?" T-Gutta asked.

"He's doing great. I want to see him but too much shit on my hands."

"Brah, go see him. That's why you have me to help you, dirty," T-Gutta answered.

They were in T-Gutta's den watching the Cowboys dominate the Dolphins, and eating some of LeLe's delicious soul food.

"Yeah, I know, but, T-Gutta, we all move together. There's too much shit going on to leave y'all niggas for a second."

"But that's yo' brother, man. I ain't hearing that shit. These streets gonna still be here when you come back, and your second-in-command, brah. Go see ya brother!" T-Gutta exclaimed.

"Alright, brah. I'll do that," Real yielded. Then from the corner of his eye he saw movement.

At first he thought it was LeLe, until he looked and saw Bellda standing at the door. Real angrily turned to T-Gutta, who immediately defended himself with his hands up.

"I swear, brah. I have nothing to do with this," T-Gutta said.

"Why is she even here?" Real asked T-Gutta.

"Because she's my company and someone who really loves you, Real. She never—" LeLe started.

"I got this, LeLe. He can run all he wants after he hears what I have to say now!" Bellda shouted with arms crossed, stepping in the way of Real, who tried to dash out of the den. Bellda was adamant about not letting him pass.

"Bellda, please! I'ma tell you this—"

Before Real could get the words out of his mouth, Bellda aggressively attacked him, planting her lips to his and forcing him to kiss her. The taste of their past flashed before him. She tasted like the Bellda that he loved and not the Bellda who had lied to him from the beginning of their relationship. All she had to do was remain true from the beginning. It was ineffable to Bellda as to why she held back about her and Pat's relationship.

Why couldn't she be real with me? What else do I not know about her? Real thought as he pulled away from her. "Why? You had a chance from day one to tell me 'bout you and that nigga!" Real exploded.

Bellda was speechless. All she could do was cry. She just couldn't explain why she had hidden her past with Pat. "Real, I'm sorry. Like for real, Jermaine! I know I fucked up!"

"And that was the biggest mistake. It's cardinal; and like a nigga I handle in these streets, there are no second chances. We done!" Real said impudently as he stormed away from Bellda, leaving her hurt, and alone with his final words.

When Real was gone, Bellda was unable to stop the steady flow of tears, and she broke down like never before. She knew that there was no getting her man back, and that he had moved on to the next bitch, Mookie.

Bellda knew all about Mookie and Real's affair, and how numerous times turned into every night. She caught Mookie's car in his driveway, and she once caught her and Real kissing and being cozy together.

But how, when he became my world? Bellda thought as T-Gutta and LeLe consoled her in a warming embrace.

* * *

"Umm, shit!" Lala moaned in ecstasy as Birdman long-stroked her from the back.

So much built-up sexual frustration between them had finally exploded. Lala and Birdman were constantly arguing about the smallest things. Today their fighting converted to making love. Birdman loved Lala to death and only wanted her to see that it was unconditional. On the other hand, Lala wanted out, but it wasn't feasible. She wanted to end their love and move on to another life. Her girl Katina had encouraged her, and now she was ready to make her move. But the dicking Birdman was laying on her had clogged her vision. She didn't want to let go of some parts of Birdman.

"Damn! I hate you!" Lala purred as she came to her orgasm shaking convulsively.

"I love you too, baby girl," Birdman exclaimed, shooting his seed inside her.

Exhausted, the duo collapsed on the bed covered in each other's sweat and body fluids.

"What makes you hate me when I'm here for you showing you I care, Lala?" Birdman asked as Lala cuddled up against him and rubbed his huge stomach.

"I don't hate you, baby. I just don't know where this is heading."

"What you mean, baby? I'm here, and I love you. We fight over the stupidest things ever. Sometimes I wonder if you're looking for a way out!" Birdman said.

He feels it. Shit! I make it obvious, Lala thought.

"If you're looking for a way out, Lala, let's go out as friends and not on bad terms. We could be better than that," Birdman explained.

Lala was at a loss for words. Why would I hurt him, especially after all he does for Destiny? I can't hurt him, but damn, he's not Real! Lala thought as she got up and looked Birdman in his eyes. *Oh, my God! He's crying,* Lala thought, immediately feeling horrible about her anticipation about leaving him.

"I'm sorry if I've hurt you. Please don't cry in front of me."

"Lala, I love you, woman," Birdman expressed as a river of tears cascaded down his face. He unabashedly cried in front of her.

Lala climbed on top of him and kissed his lips. She kissed him deep and passionately. When she looked at Birdman, she saw the gift that God had sent to her. She had her own money to take care of herself and Destiny, but to live without love genuinely was another token. If Real refused to love her like she wanted, she had someone who would.

The sententious saying is, "What you don't do, the next nigga will," Lala thought. *Birdman genuinely loves me, so why must I hurt him? I've made up my mind, and I'm taking a rest season from cracking Uncle Sam on his head. While I do that, I'll move to Tampa. I can't do him like this,* Lala finalized.

"Baby, move with me to Tampa," Lala said to Birdman while rubbing his beard.

"So that's what's been on your mind—Tampa?" he asked.

"Yes, baby. I can't raise Destiny down here. It's too dangerous, and I can't stand to lose my child to one of these inexperienced, shooting-ass niggas! I only have one!"

Birdman didn't need to hear anything else. He artistically flipped Lala over on her back and stared into her eyes.

"Woman, you became my day when it was night, and I'll never forget that. I watched you grow into a beautiful, intelligent woman, and now you are mine. I know you still feel for Real. I'll never be able to take away y'all's past. I remember you two running around like love bugs, hand in hand. I respect that nigga. That's why I fill his spot perfectly, and I wouldn't let any kind of harm come to you or my stepdaughter. When I say I love you, Lala—woman—I love you. Yes, I will go to Tampa with you. If that's what you seriously want to do, then let's do this!" Birdman exclaimed and deeply kissed Lala.

I have my king and the man who will treat me queenly. Running him off would have been a big mistake, Lala thought as she reached down and guided him inside her wet pussy.

"Umm!" Lala moaned out when Birdman plunged inside her and beat her pussy slowly and passionately.

"I love you, woman. You hear me?"

"Yes, baby! I hear you!" Lala purred.

She kissed Birdman as tears of joy cascaded down her face.

My king! she thought.

They made love until nightfall and then went to the beach for a romantic walk. It was official. Birdman was everything she was looking for—the man to fulfill the emptiness that Real had left her with.

* * *

"Damn, my nigga! How long it gonna take you to find yo' hand? If you don't have it, you don't have it!" Phat Whinny said to his homeboy Bruna.

They were playing poker under the tree at Jake's store with five other players. The game was called seven-card pick, and whoever built the best hand was the winner. Whinny and Bruna were neck and neck with four cards showing a royal flush possibly on the way.

"Man, you ain't got nothing in the hole, nigga. Hit me, Coy!" Bruna said, discarding two of his cards to gain two new ones off the deck.

"That's where you fucked—!"

Boc! Boc! Boc! Boc!

The surprise shots came out of nowhere and hit Phat Whinny in his chest, dropping him to his death. Everyone went crazy trying to run from the shots coming from the passing SUV. Bruna and a couple of his homies quickly returned fire along with Coy.

Boom! Boom! Boom!

Chop! Chop! Chop! Chop!

V-Money came running out of the store with his AK-47 and dumped at the fleeing SUV that quickly turned left on Palm Beach Road.

"Let's go!" Bruna shouted, jumping into his box Chevy Caprice in an attempt to go after the SUV.

When he turned on Palm Beach Road, he cautioned at every stop sign in search of the SUV, but to no avail.

"Shit!" Bruna exclaimed, hammering on the steering wheel when he saw the police lights behind him.

He had three of his soldiers in the car with him, and they were all strapped with drugs and their guns.

"Man, I can't stop. Y'all niggas need to jump out if y'all dirty!" Bruna said as she slowed to a stop.

Everyone except Bruna jumped out after he slid his gun and his pill bottle full of crack cocaine to his soldier Lil Dirt.

"Let's go now, crackas!" Bruna said as he smashed on the gas initiating a high-speed chase. Bruna played the game smart. He was ready to go to jail for fleeing from authorities rather than for drugs and a gun. Bruna turned left at the dead end of Palm Beach Road on 10th Street and was met with a road blocked by Martin County sheriffs. He stopped abruptly and stared at the police with their guns drawn and aimed at him.

"Get the fuck out of the car with your hands up!" a police officer exclaimed over his loud mic. "You have five seconds or we will shoot for our own safety!"

Bruna put his Chevy into park, opened the door, and then slowly stepped out. He made the mistake of trying to pull up his pants, and immediately felt a storm of bullets riddle his body.

Boom! Boom! Boc! Boc! Boc! Boom! Boc! Boc!

The Martin County police and plain-clothed officers took no chances, since they were in a high-crime neighborhood. Bruna's body hit the ground, and the last thing he could remember before taking his last breath was that he forgot to put his hands up.

SEVENTEEN

"Two dead and four in critical condition" was the news in the Treasure Coast. Real had lost two good niggas, and he was deeply disturbed. The killing of Bruna by the police led to a tumultuous protest that quickly turned into a violent riot between civilians in Indiantown and the police. Over one hundred civilians were arrested, beaten, and interrogated.

"Black lives matter! Justice for Martin!" the crowd on 10th Street shouted in protest.

"My baby! He didn't have no gun!" Bruna's wife, Toya, shouted on television.

"This shit crazy!" Real said to V-Money, who was sitting in his chair behind the counter of the store watching a news update.

V-Money changed the channel and sighed.

"Whinny dead, Bruna, Jake, Joc, and Meat Head. It goes on and on, brah. We got to find these niggas Chub and Black. We get these niggas, and the rest bowing down, brah, feel me?" Real spoke.

"So, what we gonna do?" T-Gutta asked.

"We gonna go get this nigga and bed this nigga's family and everybody affiliated. We gonna flip that shit!" Real exclaimed, wiping tears from his eyes.

I didn't plan to lose my niggas when I planned to take over. Damn! Real thought, with a heavy burden of guilt.

"Don't worry, brah," T-Gutta said, squeezing Real's shoulder to comfort him. "We gonna got get these niggas

Black and Big Chub. We gonna go until we got this fucking nigga's mama eating dirt."

* * *

Crazy Zoe and Boxhead looked at the news going down in the swamp. They were eager to return and hit more of the Swamp Mafia. The sight of mourning excited Crazy Zoe. Big Chub celebrated with them. He knew that the more blood Crazy Zoe saw, the more hyped up he became.

He would drink his enemy's blood if he could! Big Chub thought while watching Crazy Zoe attentively watching the news.

"That nigga Real not showing his face. What kind of god is he?" Crazy Zoe exclaimed.

"A smart, very extraordinary, and prudent one!" Big Chub explained, taking a sip of his glass of Remy Martin.

"What you mean?" Crazy Zoe asked, feeling like Big Chub had given an enemy too much credit. It just didn't sit well with Crazy Zoe, who placed Real beneath his feet.

"Like I meant it to mean. It will take forever if you're looking for an easy kill, Haitian," Big Chub explained. "Polo definitely has him protected. We're at war, Crazy, not playing a card game. Your move has to be five moves ahead if you want Real."

Big Chub stood up and walked over toward the minibar where Crazy Zoe was sitting.

"Tell me, why did you two go and shoot up Jake's store?" Big Chub inquired, pointing at Boxhead and Crazy Zoe.

"Shit! To make them niggas pay the price, brah. What other reason?" Crazy Zoe said.

"What about you, Boxhead?" Big Chub asked.

"Shit! We went to hit them niggas up because it was tit-for-tat, like Crazy said."

Big Chub looked at both of his soldiers and was very disappointed. He shook his head, which deeply perplexed Crazy Zoe and Boxhead.

"Wrong! Damn it!" Big Chub exploded, pounding his fist down on the bar counter.

"We hit them targets because a real nigga will show at his nigga's funeral, right?" Big Chub asked, with his palms upside down. "And when we put a king in check, he has to get out of check, right? Unless it's checkmate, right?"

Now I see what he's hitting on, Crazy Zoe and his brother both thought.

"So we about to light this nigga up at the wake, huh?" Boxhead asked.

"Exactly. Now we're on the same page. And if we miscalculate and he somehow slides out of check, we threaten his most powerful piece: his queen!" Big Chub exclaimed.

* * *

The next day Real left T-Gutta in command of the streets while he and Johnny took a trip to go see Shamoney. After they were cleared and walked through the doors of the visitation lobby, a retrospection of when he was doing time hit Real. Shamoney had never gotten a chance to come visit him during his bid due to him having close-range felonies and being too caught up in the streets. On the other hand, Johnny had stopped coming to see Real when he turned eighteen and he was no longer forced by his mother, Michele, to come.

"This place got better bitches working here than Martin. I can say that for sure!" Real said to Johnny while sitting at the table waiting for Shamoney to come out.

"Yeah, I remember good. All the hos at Martin Correctional were dykes with bigger dicks than both of us put together," Johnny retorted.

"Nigga, yo' ass a clown!" Real laughed, catching eye contact with one of the pretty-ass female guards.

"Man, shorty all in yo' grill, brah. Go ahead and see what she 'bout," Johnny said, encouraging Real to go put his mack game down. "Go, nigga! What! You scared?" Johnny joked.

"Hell no, nigga! Watch this shit!" Real responded. "I'ma go grab some food for brah so it'll be hot before he gets here. It might be an hour before Shamoney gets cleared," Real retorted as he strutted off.

When Real was gone, Johnny wiped away the perspiration forming on his forehead. "I can't believe I'm doing this," he mumbled to himself.

Johnny was wearing a small wire attached to his Polo shirt. When Real had asked why he was dressed like he was going to a funeral, he replied that he was just feeling himself. The FBI, DEA, and ATF were all tuned in listening to their entire conversation.

I could tell brah to drop me off in Georgia, and make a run for it . . . I can't. Them crackas would definitely get my ass. If I give them Real, I could take over the streets and still be a free nigga. That I'd rather do! Johnny thought in his own little world.

When he looked up, he saw Shamoney looking for his visitors. Johnny whistled to get his attention.

"Yo, damn! You the last person I would think of seeing!" Shamoney exclaimed as he jumped into his brother's arms and

148

hugged him tightly, like it was his last hug on earth. "Damn, brah. It feels like it's been forever since I seen you!" Shamoney said.

"Boo!" Real said from behind Shamoney.

Shamoney turned around and saw his eldest brother standing with an arm full of food. Real laid down the food on the table and then embraced his brother, giving him a pound on his back.

"Damn, brah! It's good to see you hanging in there!" Real said, excited to see his brother.

"Y'all niggas surprised me, and Chantele ain't even tell me shit!" Shamoney said as he sat down.

"You getting your swole on I see," Real said.

"Nigga, I run this prison. I got this pad on lock. Hos, dope, you name it," Shamoney bragged.

"We already know that. So who that thick-ass ho with the buzz cut?" Real asked Shamoney.

"Oh, that's my boo's bitch."

"Man, tell her a nigga got all that she missing. Shorty got a phat ass on her, man!" Real exclaimed.

"I'll see what she has to say. If it's a go, she'll call you. The shorty next to her is her bitch, Sgt. Thomas, my boo," Shamoney introduced Real to his sideline bitch.

"She give up the pussy?" Johnny asked.

"I ain't callin' her my bitch if she ain't, lil brah, feel me?"

"Man, let's get this picture out of the way so we can chill," Real said as he stood up.

He wanted everything out of the way before he broke the news to Shamoney about what was going on in the hood. He told Chantele not to tell him anything. He wanted to be the one to break the news to Shamoney. The trio took five pictures together while a new Haitian in the compound named Bozo looked on with pure hatred in his heart for all of them.

* * *

When Lunatic pulled up to the trap in East Stuart where T-Gutta was preparing one hundred kilos of cocaine to get put on the tow truck, he bumped into one of his workers.

"What's good, Yez?" Lunatic asked, stepping out of his newest Monte Carlo.

"Shit! Just take it slow, brah. I got like four more ounces of that brick you gave me. A nigga gonna swallow that shit tonight as soon as my cracka come through," Yez said.

Yez was a red-skinned nigga who stood five eight and weighed 185 pounds. He had a mouth full of golds. He was Lunatic's sergeant in the East Stuart area, and he controlled Bahama Street.

"Shit! Give me an hour, and I'll make sure I leave you with something before I take it in," Lunatic said.

"Already?" Yez exclaimed.

"Brah, you see any fishy shit, bust first and talk later," Lunatic informed Yez.

Lunatic walked off and entered the trap house with his key. When he stepped inside, he saw three butt-naked female workers helping T-Gutta put the cooked bricks inside a duffel bag. T-Gutta's iPhone rang, and it was one of his clients to whom he owed two bricks. They had driven down from Orlando just to pick them up.

"Brah, I'ma need you to handle this while I go make a quick sell around the corner," T-Gutta explained to Lunatic, placing him in charge.

"Go ahead and handle business, brah. I got it," Lunatic said.

"Appreciate it!" T-Gutta responded.

T-Gutta grabbed two bricks, placed them inside a towel, and walked out the front door. "Yo, Yez!" T-Gutta called.

"Yeah, what's up, brah?"

"I need you to keep an eye on any wrong movement. If you see it, handle it," T-Gutta instructed.

"I got ya, brah! All ready!" Yez retorted.

"Alright," T-Gutta said as he hopped in his Range Rover and sped away with two birds on the passenger seat.

* * *

Lunatic quickly helped the workers store the kilos inside the duffel bags. Altogether there were one hundred being trafficked out and going along the East Coast per routine. Lunatic walked to the freezer to remove the last four kilos when he heard gunshots close by.

Boc! Boc! Boc!

"FBI! Get down!" Lunatic heard loud and clear.

He took a look at the frightened workers, pulled out his Glock .40, and rushed to the door. He locked the door and then looked out the window.

"Shit!" Lunatic exclaimed after seeing the FBI surrounding the house.

There was no way out. Frustrated and angry, Lunatic turned the gun on the female workers and squeezed the trigger.

Boom! Boom! Boom!

Lunatic shot all three workers at close range in their heads, killing them instantly as he rushed to the hallway closet and pulled down an AR-15 from the top shelf. He racked it and then prepared to take on Martin County sheriffs, FBI, DEA, whoever. He was ready to go out in style.

"This is the FBI. Please come out of the house with your hands up. Surrender your weapon, or we will come in."

Bop! Bop! Bop! Bop! Bop! Bop!

Before Agent Swells could finish trying to negotiate with Lunatic, shots came out of the living room window, hitting a couple of unmarked cars.

"We have all day to play this game, and in the end, we will still win," Agent Swells announced.

* * *

When T-Gutta got the call from Lunatic, he couldn't believe his ears until he saw the stand-off with his own eyes. He couldn't drive down Bayou Street because the FBI had the road completely blocked off.

"I'm scared, brah. I ain't even gonna lie to you. Everybody is slumped. They think I have a hostage. I can't go nowhere!" Lunatic began crying on the phone to T-Gutta. "Brah, we been down for a minute. We've done a lot of shit together. Why it got to end like this?" Lunatic cried.

"Listen, brah!"

Boom!

"No, Tic!" T-Gutta cried out for Lunatic but got no answer.

He felt it in his gut. It was over.

Lunatic was gone, and T-Gutta knew it. It was further confirmed when the FBI rammed down the front door and came out empty-handed. The last thing Lunatic planned on doing was going to prison for the rest of his life.

"Damn! Lunatic. Fuck!" T-Gutta cried in the front seat of his Range Rover.

Yez and a couple more soldiers were arrested nearby. Despite Yez taking a couple hits from Agent Swells's Glock 9 mm, none of the shots were fatal.

"Damn it!" T-Gutta exclaimed, banging his hand on the steering wheel as he quickly got away from the scene.

* * *

Real wasn't liking the news about Lunatic one bit. Another homeboy down in one week. Lunatic was his childhood homie. It was difficult for Real to drive safely to Georgia to drop off fifty kilos hidden in a stash spot in the Chevy Tahoe SUV, so he let Johnny drive the short distance to Atlanta. When they arrived, Johnny pulled around back of Club Magic and waited for the two bouncers he knew to come out the back door.

"What's up, J?" the six five, 250-pound bouncer said to Johnny.

"What's new, soldier?" Johnny replied.

"You do remember my brother, don't you, B.B.?" Real asked.

"Of course, we do," Sam, the other bouncer, answered.

"Well, let's get business done. We're in a hurry. It's urgent for us to get back," Real spoke.

"Alright, boss. We can do that as quickly as possible. We wouldn't want to keep you guys waiting all day," B.B. answered.

No less than five minutes later, the money was brought out to Real and Johnny in a duffel bag, and the transaction was made.

"Nice doing business with you guys. I swear you've helped us put Atlanta on the map for real. We'll be down to check out Club 772 when we get off this load. Instead of y'all driving, is it okay if we bring the re-up money and traffic our shit back? Deal?" Sam asked.

"Sealed!" Real retorted, finalizing the deal.

Real was in Tallahassee three hours later, and he still could not believe that Lunatic was gone. Much as he didn't want it to be true, he knew that all the condolences he had seen on Facebook were genuine.

Damn, Lunatic! Real thought.

He was exhausted in his vagrant thoughts, trying to find the snake, not knowing it that the man he called "little brother" was highly responsible for the sudden mayhem occurring in East Stuart.

No doubt there's a weak link, but how can I find it and destroy him or her? Real thought, not knowing who to trust.

* * *

Agents Davis and Smalls were disappointed in how Agent Swells led the takedown.

"He paused up when he was supposed to continue. He was supposed to take the damn door down!" Agent Smalls said angrily.

Davis had never seen Smalls so furious. She strongly disliked Swells and thought that his veteran fat ass should be somewhere running a donut shop rather than being an FBI agent one more day. Not only were both agents furious, but Director Johnson was not liking it one bit either.

Swells has caused havoc and isn't the hero that he's portrayed to be, Smalls thought.

"Everything was running smoothly until he chickened out and let the muthafucka blow his brains out. Coward is what he is! If it was me and you, we would have had Lunatic's ass spilling red beans everywhere by now," Smalls expressed, sitting in the passenger seat while Davis drove back to headquarters in Martin County.

"We're still under the radar. No one knows where this hit came from," Davis said.

"Yeah, I guess you have a point!" Smalls retorted while rubbing her temple, trying to sooth away the frustration.

* * *

What Chucky and Kentucky saw surprised them. As soon as Kentucky heard from Real about what was occurring in East Stuart, he and Chucky took a drive to update Real. When Kentucky saw, Courtney walk out wearing an FBI jacket and vest with a tall gray-haired man, his heart skipped a beat.

"She's FBI. I knew something was wrong with her when Pablo couldn't find her in his data!" Kentucky explained.

"How the fuck did Real slip up, man?" Chucky questioned. "Things were going so good."

"Yeah right! This shit is crazy! She knows who we are."

"Shit!" Chucky exclaimed.

"We'll finish her and then leave. We should go now, but I can't leave Real hanging," Kentucky said.

"We'll take her out and then go back into hiding," Chucky said.

"Yeah, sounds like a plan," Kentucky retorted.

EIGHTEEN

Hearing the disturbing news of Courtney being an FBI agent made Real more furious than ever. Bad as he wanted to call an emergency meeting, he had to go with Kentucky and Chucky's advice. He needed to find the snake to lift his head up. They had summoned Real to Bathtub Beach on Hutchinson Island in the middle of the night. He left Mookie in bed asleep. They were strictly operating by text and not direct phone calls.

"I can't believe this shit, brah!" Real exclaimed.

"Put it like this, she played me. I'm sure she played Johnny too," Kentucky explained to Real.

"It now explains how they got the tip to the warehouse to raid Su'Rabbit. She bugged Johnny," Real theorized.

"Exactly! We don't know how close she was playing with him, but we need to find out. Does Johnny still talk to her? We can't blow their cover," Kentucky advised. "Since I'ma take her out, I think it's best for me to watch her closely. I feel like she's watching us now, but she can't hear shit. That's why we chose the beach," Kentucky continued. "I came to help you, Real. I'm not leaving you in this alone. But just promise me that when we clean up, run and get out of the country for awhile. Being that the FBI is involved, we're only waiting for the bomb to explode."

"Tick, tock!" Chucky added.

"Damn it, man! How the fuck did I slip up?" Real exclaimed, rubbing his face out of frustration.

"Find out if Johnny is still seeing this bitch, and then we will go from there. Until then, I'ma be watching her every move," Kentucky said, giving Real a squeeze for reassurance.

"We're in this together, Real, just like we started. We're a three-man wrecking crew," Chucky reminded him.

The trio hugged each other and then quickly dispersed, going their separate ways.

* * *

One Week Later

The Reverend Gary Church in the swamp could only hold so many people, and it was filled to capacity. Phat Whinny's and Bruna's funerals had to be held separately. Phat Whinny's service was from 10:00 a.m. until 2:00 p.m., and then Bruna's service was held from 2:30 p.m. to 6:30 p.m.

Big Chub had laid on the church for both services and was furious when he didn't see Real show up to either service.

"You think he knows that we laying on him?" Crazy Zoe asked.

"I don't know. It's hard to say," Big Chub lied.

Hell yeah, he knew we would be laying on him. That's why the nigga didn't show. He moved out of check like we expected of him! Big Chub thought.

"That's the nigga that killed Tankhead. I'll never forget his face, and he the only nigga with a shoulder sling. I know I hit that nigga. I seen him jerk," Crazy Zoe said, all hyped up. His adrenaline was racing at one hundred miles per hour. "Let me get 'em, Chub," Crazy Zoe asked for permission.

"No! We got bigger fish to fry," Big Chub said.

He drove off as church was being let out with Bruna's black casket being placed inside a hearse.

* * *

Real had listened to the prudent advice from Polo and chose not to show up at the funerals. But he did pay his respects when it was time to view the bodies. The protesting was still going for Bruna, and riots had popped off all throughout the Treasure Coast. Fort Piece, Port St. Lucie, Indian River, and Okeechobee had come together to support Black Lives Matter.

Shit was getting out of hand, and Real had the right man to get some form of satisfaction: Kentucky, his sharpshooter. In just one week, Kentucky had sniped five police and two DEA agents. It was complete mayhem. And it only got worse for the police trying to keep peace in the streets.

Real had finally gotten a chance to catch up with Johnny. For a week, Kentucky had been losing Courtney's trail only to turn around and trail her again. He was a professional with it, and the reports coming back about Johnny were not good. The FBI was definitely watching Johnny with an eagle eye. Real decided to probe his brother while they were driving in his Range Rover.

"Lil brah, what's up with you and that lil baby you snatched up from the club—the dancer? Y'all still fucking?" Real asked Johnny, who tensed up instantly but bridled himself.

"Nah, brah. I haven't seen that bitch in a minute," Johnny retorted.

Real knew he was lying because he had photos of him eating breakfast with her two days before at a Denny's in Port St. Lucie.

"Why you ask?" Johnny was curious.

"Remember when you told me that she'd let both of us hang out if the money was right?" Real reminded him.

"Yeah, I remember that. Shit! If I see her in the club this week, I'll run that by her," Johnny said as he nervously looked out the window.

Real couldn't believe his ears. Johnny had straight up lied to him, and it left him bothered. Vagrant thoughts of Johnny possibly working with the police swarmed Real's head. But despite the circumstantial evidence, Real still couldn't put it in his heart that Johnny was an informer.

* * *

"Do you think he's onto Johnny?" Smalls asked Davis as they trailed Real and Johnny and listened to their conversation.

"I think he's just horny," Davis said.

"So you got jokes, huh?" Smalls shot back, punching him in his arm.

"Hey, you asked me, and I told you what I think," Davis retorted, laughing at Smalls's face.

"I think we're doing a great job keeping you in the picture instead of me. Tonight, go to the dance club with Dirt and Johnny. I bet he believes you're that one girl who's down for the pleasure."

"How 'bout we take both of them down now."

"And give Black back his turf so he can go into hiding for another decade," Davis said. "I don't think so."

"I like you," Smalls said.

"And I love you," Davis responded.

"Are you serious?" Smalls asked, not believing her ears.

"As a heartbeat."

Without anything else to say, Smalls unfastened her seatbelt, ducked before the dashboard, and slid over to Davis. She undid his belt and pulled out his erect dick. She sucked him fast and almost caused him to swerve out of traffic. When Davis exploded, he shot his load down her gullet, where Smalls swallowed him and sucked him dry.

"Yes, I mean it. I love you, if that's what you're asking me," Davis said breathlessly.

* * *

T-Gutta had been laying low paranoid, just like Real had told him. All he could think about was his boy Lunatic. He had buried him the day before and seen him go in the ground, yet it still hadn't dawned on him that his round was gone. Alleycat had come from New York, and he too couldn't believe that Lunatic was gone—dead.

"Baby, are you ready to eat?" LeLe asked T-Gutta, who was in the den watching ESPN with his son, T.J.

"Yeah, baby, bring me and Jr. a plate. You hungry, boy?" T-Gutta asked his son, who was a Jr. from a previous relationship

T.J. was ten years old and growing up fast.

"Yes, sir."

"Well, tell your stepmother you're hungry," T-Gutta said to his son.

"Ma, can I get a plate like my daddy?" T.J. asked LeLe.

"You sure can. When you go wash your hands, mister."

"Yes, ma'am," T.J. said as he ran to the bathroom to wash his hands for dinner.

"You're stressing again, baby. I'm here for you," LeLe said as she rubbed T-Gutta on the back of his neck to soothe his frustration.

She knew he was grieving the loss of a friend, and dodging a federal indictment.

"Baby, I want you to know that I don't care what happens. We both knew the risk, and I'ma be by your side through it all," LeLe promised.

"Thanks, baby. I know you will."

* * *

As Real lay on his back and Mookie slept in his arms, all he could think about was everything going on around him.

"Hello?" Johnny's sleepy voice answered.

"What's up, lil brah?" Real asked.

"It's four o'clock in the morning, nigga. What's on your mind?"

He sounds normal, Real felt.

"Don't worry about the Georgia drop. They're coming to the club tonight."

"So, we not going up there, is what you're telling me?" Johnny asked.

"Yeah, we chilling," Real replied.

"Okay, brah."

"Where you at, my nigga?" Real asked, cutting off Johnny.

"Shit! I'm at my lil baby's house."

"Who's that, Courtney?" Real asked.

Johnny laughed a little before he spoke.

"Nah, brah. Dominique."

"My bad, brah. Well, get back at me in the morning," Real said.

161

"I'll do that, brah," Johnny retorted and then disconnected the call.

Maybe I'm overreacting. My brother is too solid, man, Real thought as his iPhone rang. Not looking at the number, he answered quickly. "Hello?"

"Real, I love you."

"Bellda, what is it that you don't get? We done! Lose my number, like seriously!"

"So, you think that ho Mookie gonna make it and fill my spot, nigga? Watch how I show you. If you can't love me, then stop fuckin' with me for almost a year."

Real quickly hung up on Bellda and thought nothing of her threats.

"That why you can't give the dick to everybody," Mookie said from behind Real, startling him a bit.

"Do you think you'd ever act like that?" Real asked as he turned around and put Mookie in his arms.

She slid her hands into his Polo briefs and slowly stroked him to an erection.

"No, I wouldn't act like that. I'd let you see how much you'll miss me, if anything. And most important, I wouldn't betray you to be in that type of situation," Mookie said as she descended and placed Real's dick in her mouth after backing him up to the sofa.

* * *

It was 6:00 a.m., and the sun didn't come up until 6:45. Lala had to be at the American Bank at 7:45 to cash her phony check. She didn't have to worry about Destiny, because she was with Lala's mother, Pernel, and Birdman was on the road trafficking for Real.

She looked at the check again and saw that it was duplicated correctly with no errors. She then called Mookie.

"Hello."

"Bitch, how'd I know you'd be up?"

"Because it's check day, bitch. I'm on my way," Mookie said.

"Okay, you know where I'm at."

"I'm not home, but I'll be there, boo."

"Damn, let me find out! Your boo thang wifeyin' you up?" Lala asked.

"Please don't. I won't hear the last of it."

And you'll kill both of us, Mookie wanted to tell Lala so badly, but could not.

Mookie was too far in, and she didn't care how Lala would take it if and when she did find out that she was fucking the man she so badly wanted back in her life.

"Okay, I'll spare you. Sooner or later he'll show himself," Lala said.

"Of course he will. I'll call you soon, Lala," Mookie said before hanging up the phone.

Today Lala went on a spree to cash duplicated checks at banks. She and Mookie were partners, as were Pimp and Luscious. They cashed checks on the West Coast, while Lala and Mookie took the East Coast.

"Let's go get this money, baby!" Lala said as she rolled up her kush blunt and waited for Mookie to show up.

* * *

Shamoney only got up for breakfast on days when they served "shit on the shank." Today he stayed in bed, since it was pancake day. He hated pancakes with a passion because

Central Correctional served pancakes all the time. His cellmate, Strong, hopped up to go get breakfast. He respectfully did his hygiene out in the dayroom so that he wouldn't wake up Shamoney.

"Inmates, Zone 1 get ready for chow. Please file out in the sally port," Sgt. Thomas's voice boomed over the loud PA system.

When Shamoney heard her voice, he knew that she would come to his cell per usual to get a quick fuck from Shamoney. He smiled, anticipating her arrival.

Shamoney played possum while listening to the last inmate slam the door.

They are all out in the sally port now, Shamoney thought as he turned on his back and pulled his dick through the slot of his boxers.

He heard a door slam.

That's her, come on and give me some of that good pussy, Shamoney thought.

He heard his cell door being pulled back. He kept his eyes closed and waited for her to come up to him and put his dick in her mouth. Instead of feeling Sgt. Thomas's mouth, Shamoney felt a sharp object pierce through his throat. When his eyes shot open, he saw a muscular silhouette standing over him. As Shamoney held onto his throat with a sixteen-inch shank piercing through and blood spilling from his neck, he heard Sgt. Thomas come over the PA system: "Hurry up, Bozo!"

Why? Shamoney thought as he took his last breath.

"Haitian mafia came long ways to yank!" Bozo said as he stabbed Shamoney's corpse twenty more times before he made a successful exit with the help of Sgt. Thomas.

NINETEEN

Michele never called Real over to her house and used the word "emergency." When Real made it there and saw all the family cars parked behind each other, he knew something was seriously wrong.

"What's going on, Tiffany?" Real asked his cousin, whose eyes were puffy and red from crying.

Tiffany opened her mouth, but when she tried to speak, no words came out.

"Cuz!" Tiffany tried to begin before she broke down again.

"Man, somebody tell me something!" Real shouted as he made a dash to the front door and entered the house.

Everyone was gathered in the den around his mother, and it only frightened Real with burning curiosity.

Something wrong with my ma? Real thought as he broke through the circle of his aunties and uncles.

"Ma, what's going on? You okay?" Real asked his mother, afraid to get an answer.

"Son, we lost Shada," Michele broke down in Real's auntie's arms.

"What?" Real whispered. He didn't want to believe what he had just heard, but he knew his mom well enough to know she wouldn't play death games on her kids.

"What you mean we lost Shamoney? Ma, tell me something!" Real demanded before completely losing it when he heard the loud shrill of Chantele crying.

"Noo!" Chantele cried out from the living room.

* * *

Black and Big Chub were enjoying the news of Shamoney's assassination. It was music to the Haitian mafia's ears when Bozo called with the secret code that the mafia used to signify mission completed.

"The gods have prevailed!" Bozo relayed to Big Chub.

"Unc, I can't believe he's gone myself!" Big Chub said.

"The gods have prevailed, nephew," Black said in Creole.

"Yes, they have," Big Chub answered.

Black picked up his phone and dialed a number he knew off the top of his head.

"Speak, Haitian!" Polo's voice picked up on the second ring.

"When a lion is feeble and hurt on the inside, what is left of him that makes him a mighty lion?" Black asked Polo, and then began laughing impishly.

"I remember this one. The roar, huh?" Polo said in Creole.

"Polo, you know that your lion can't beat the master at his own game. You be sure to tell Real that the only way I'ma stop aiming at family is when he yields and steps down from his own power."

"Ah huh. So you admitting that the lion is mighty?" Polo asked.

"Listen to me good, Polo. Your best bet is to call off your lion and for you to stay in retirement."

"What 'bout you, Black? Are you going to stay running as a wanted man? It seems like the smartest man that should be in retirement is you!" Polo retorted.

"Polo, listen. You know how the game is with me. Until I kill every yank, I will let the gods handle my lightweight," Black responded.

"Are you sure the gods still know your name? Last I checked, you had no love for the gods," Polo said to Black before he disconnected the phone.

"Of course the gods remember my name. How do you think I was able to give them Shamoney's soul?" Black said to him and himself and Big Chub.

* * *

Everyone was calling Real's phone and trying to send their condolences, but he wasn't picking up. Real was even ignoring Mookie's calls and sending her straight to voice mail. He had no conversation for the world. He needed time to think about all that was going on around him. He didn't have the solid proof, but he had his instincts. His gut feeling told him that Black, the invisible man, was behind killing his brother, who was stabbed twenty-one times, twenty of those which he didn't he feel.

Talk to me, 'Money. Who did this to you? Real spoke to himself.

"Somebody knows what happened to you, brah. And I'ma find out who knows," Real cried, grieving as he took another swig of Remy Martin.

Real's phone rang, and he saw that it was Kentucky, the man with whom he needed to talk.

"Hello?" Real answered sluggishly, inebriated from too much liquor.

"Good news or bad?" Kentucky inquired.

"Bad news," Real chose.

"It's official about what we're looking into," Kentucky said, tossing Real a curveball about Johnny dealing with the FBI. "Good news is it can be handled. I say we handle buddy on your own clock, but he makes it easy for us to handle the other problem."

"I will decide on this when I'm sober. How's Frank?" Real asked about Chucky.

"He left safely before the sun," Kentucky said.

"Okay, good. Just give me a couple hours," Real said.

"Brah, take all day. I'm out here. I love you, brah!" Kentucky said.

"I love you too, brah!" Real sincerely retorted before hanging up.

Johnny's working with the police, huh?

"Damn it, Johnny!" Real exploded, throwing the Remy bottle to the ground and shattering it to pieces.

* * *

Bellda was at work and couldn't get through to Real. On her break, she tried him again but still got no answer. She wanted him to know that she was still there for him as a friend. She talked to Chantele and gave her condolences to her, and she promised when she got off from working a double that she would be there to sit with her.

Bellda felt sorry for Chantele, and all she could think about was her gratefulness that it wasn't Real. She wouldn't know what to do if she lost him.

I don't think I could stomach the loss of Real. Lord, what has this man done to me? Why can't I accept that I lost him? Bellda thought as a tear rolled from her right eye.

She was in pain, and the only person that could relieve her anguish was Real.

But now he's so in love with Mookie, a cutthroat-ass bitch who has no loyalty for her friends, Bellda thought. *I dragged*

Lala's ass, and I'll drag her ass too! That ho got something that belongs to me, and I'ma have her ass. Fuck this chill mode shit!

Her break was over, and it was time to go back to work.

Bellda texted LeLe as she walked back into the building: "We need to talk when I get off!"

* * *

Mookie stayed outside in the car while Lala went inside the bank to cash her check. They were in Orlando and had been taking turns at multiple banks on the way up the East Coast of Florida.

While Lala was in the bank, Mookie once again tried to get a hold of Real. "Come on, man. Pick up!" she said as she persistently listened to the phone ring.

He's not answering for no one! Mookie thought with frustration.

Their next step was the bank in Tampa, and they had only two checks to cash. Mookie couldn't wait to get back to Martin County so she could be there for Real during his hardship and grieving period.

I'm supposed to be there by him through it all. I'm already staying with him every night.

"What the fuck!" Mookie exclaimed when she saw all the police surrounding the bank.

Fidgeting with her phone, she tried calling Lala, who was not picking up.

"Girl, get the fuck out of there!" Mookie screamed as she became paranoid while starting up her Charger. "Come on, Lala! Get out of there," Mookie said, and again tried calling, but to no avail. So she tried sending her a text: "Police! Get out!"

When Mookie raised her head and looked toward the bank, she saw that the Charger they had rented was surrounded by Orlando sheriffs and two plain-clothed detectives, who were aiming their Glock 21s at her. Mookie was scared.

"Ma'am, step out of the car with your hands up. Please don't do anything stupid!" the redneck detective demanded.

Mookie did exactly as she was told. As she was being handcuffed behind her back, she saw Lala being led out of the bank and taken to a Chevy Tahoe SUV.

Where the fuck did we go wrong? Mookie thought as the detectives led her to another unmarked Tahoe.

She couldn't see Lala from the tent, but she could feel Lala probing her mind with the same question: *Where did we go wrong?*

* * *

Pimp and Luscious made it back to the swamp on time and were surprised to see that Lala and Mookie hadn't returned yet, and they weren't picking up their phones.

"It's not like them to not pick up. Neither of them is picking up!" Pimp said while sitting at her kitchen table counting the $30,000 they had accumulated from hitting multiple banks on the West Coast.

"Maybe they in a no-service zone," Pimp suggested.

"I pray that it's not nothing other than that!" Luscious said, relaxing on the comfortable sofa in Pimp's living room.

"So, what we wearing to the club?" Pimp asked Luscious while she sat at her kitchen table full of money.

"I was thinking we all just leopard it out! I got a catsuit, so that'll make all the boys come to the yard," Luscious said.

"Oh yeah, well where did you get it from?" Pimp asked.

"That's too much information. If I tell you, I'll have to kill you!" Luscious exclaimed.

"Girl, what the fuck is going on? They're still not picking up. Do you have Katina's number? Maybe they headed over to her spot. Tampa was their last spot. That's what she told me," Pimp said.

"I don't have her number, but I can Facebook her," Luscious said.

"Do that while I go take a shower. When I'm done, we heading over to your house," Pimp said as she strutted off.

She was ready to see V-Money tonight. She was dick-starving and in need of some real hardcore sex. She was ready to be called every dirty name in the book. As she showered, Pimp's mind went to Shamoney. It just didn't seem real to her that he was killed in prison. Her heart went out to Real and his family. Shamoney would surely be missed.

This shit is crazy how a nigga here one moment and gone the next! Pimp said to herself in the shower. *Where the fuck are Lala and Mookie?*

* * *

Kentucky had made it to the top of an abandoned building under construction in Martin County across the street from the courthouse. It was where he lost the FBI. Courtney trailed him. He knew she hated when he played that game with her. Now it was his time to watch. He carried a black backpack on his back with his favorite sniper gun—an M-110, which was faster than a .300 Win. Mag. bolt action. He was skilled enough to hit a bullseye three hundred yards away and faster than an eye blink.

He had seen Courtney and her partner walk into the courthouse with another agent. Johnny had just exited the car with them, and then he hopped into a cab. Looking at the sky, Kentucky saw that a downpour was on its way, so he just sat down and waited. It was now a waiting game as he sat in the ready position.

Rushing to the courthouse to get a warrant signed was a headache, but it was routine, and they had their probable cause to search and seize all property associated with Travon "T-Gutta" Jamison. Johnny had given the scope on T-Gutta, and now it was time to move in and take down everyone affiliated with the Swamp Mafia.

Agents Davis, Smalls, and Swells waited patiently for Judge Leven to overlook the merits of the warrant in his chambers, and sign.

"Why is it taking forever?" Smalls whispered to Davis and Swells.

"Only in Martin County. If we were in Dade, then this wouldn't be a problem," Swells exclaimed, pacing outside with his hands behind his back while the trio waited for the bailiff to come announce the judge's presence.

"Where do you think Mr. Dirt went off to this time?" Smalls asked.

"I wish I could tell you," Davis returned, sitting on the bench next to a hunched-over Smalls.

"So we get the warrant signed, and we take him down the moment we see that he's home. Then we take down Markee Anderson with the 4-Life circle," Agent Smalls explained.

"Sounds like a plan, but I still want to wait out the funeral. You heard Real. He feels that Black is responsible for the death of his brother," Davis explained.

"So just like a fly's attracted to shit, let's see how bold Black gets!" Smalls suggested.

"We could do that. It'll be a good move. Let's see what we get, and then after the funeral, we move in!" Davis exclaimed.

It was ten minutes before the judge returned and signed the search warrant for Travon Jamison. The agents then walked out together in the heavy rain.

"Damn it! There was no sign of rain!" Smalls shouted.

"I'll be soaking wet—!"

Crack!

Before he could say another word, Swells's head exploded from a sniper's shot. Davis and Smalls quickly drew their weapons and ducked, trying to find the shooter's location.

Crack!

Another shot took down Smalls, knocking the wind out of her as the vest stopped the bullet. The pain was horrible, and all she could remember before things went black was Davis standing over her screaming into his walkie-talkie for backup.

"FBI down! East Ocean Boulevard courthouse. We have a sniper."

Crack!

"Aww!" Davis screamed in pain, going down to his knee when a bullet pierced his thigh.

He's going to kill me! Davis thought as he fell into unconsciousness.

Kentucky took off.

TWENTY

Tock!

When Kentucky made it down from the construction site, he jogged over to 3rd Street and hopped into his rented Dodge Durango. As he left, Martin County sheriffs quickly rushed over to the courthouse.

"That'll keep ya down and out of my business," Kentucky said as he accelerated to Real's place.

* * *

It was crazy. Real had received a call from Lala and Mookie from the Orlando County Jail. Both of them had no bond until they saw a first-appearance judge in the morning. They were separated and on different floors, and they were both asking for his help. Lala was Birdman's full responsibility, but if Birdman couldn't bring Lala home, Real would, out of the kindness of his heart.

Tonight, Real had business to handle, and it was out of town. When Kentucky pulled up, he hopped inside the Dodge Durango with Kentucky and took the wheel. His Georgia connect was on his way to pick up product. And just like Real had planned, he was five moves ahead of the FBI and his own brother as he was in the wind.

"Man, I wish you would have seen how I broke down that gray-headed muthafucka!" Kentucky said, demonstrating to Real how he had taken the FBI off his trail.

Kentucky was funny while acting out his moves, and Real loved him like a brother. That's why he couldn't let anybody deal with Johnny but him.

I can't believe you, Johnny. You went out like a straight busta! Real thought, bridling his emotions.

* * *

When Agent Smalls came around, she was in the back of an ambulance and slightly dizzy.

"Welcome aboard," Agent Sullivan said, standing in the doorway.

Her chest was on fire—a pain searing through her entire body.

"Where's Davis?" Smalls asked.

"He was rushed to ER!"

"What's wrong with him?" Agent Smalls asked, showing her deep concern for her partner.

"The sniper decided to play 'Eeny, Meeny, Miny, Moe' with you guys."

"Oh my gosh! I remember. Swells is dead, isn't he?" Smalls asked, already knowing the answer.

"Yep! I'm afraid there was nothing we could do for Swells. He was moe," Agent Sullivan retorted.

"How bad is Davis?" Smalls asked, looking around at the crime scene at the courthouse.

"Who snipes three agents at the courthouse?" Sullivan asked, trying to fish for information.

"We know damn well who would do it!" Smalls said to him as she stepped out of the ambulance.

When she looked on the floor of the ambulance, she saw her lifesaver—her vest. Picking it up and inspecting the bullet dent, she thanked God for making vests, after seeing the shot lined up with her heart.

"He's good, ain't he?" Sullivan asked as it began lightly raining again.

"I have to get to Davis."

"No! You have to get to headquarters to speak with Director Johnson. He's waiting on you," Sullivan said, throwing shade back in Smalls's face.

Agent Smalls caught onto his sarcasm.

"Fuck you, jackass!" Smalls retorted as she grabbed her damaged vest and then strutted off to her unmarked car.

Before getting inside, she looked toward the front door of the courthouse and saw Swells's body under a shroud.

"Damn it, Swells! You didn't deserve this!" Smalls said to herself as she went to headquarters to see her boss.

"I just hope Davis is okay, Lord!" she said as she came to an intersection at a red light.

I can't believe I've fallen for this man. My dad warned me about dating older men. Everything my equal in age would fail, they would ace. And Davis is my ace, Smalls thought as the light turned green.

She flicked on her red and blue lights and ran through every light until she arrived at headquarters.

* * *

When Real and Kentucky pulled up to the trap house in Palm Beach, Capo and Juvie opened the door for them. Sitting in a chair bound by rope, with duct tape over his mouth, was a Haitian mafia Zoe named King Zoe. On the floor was Poppa with his brains blown out of his head. This was Juvie's butcher pad. Trap Money and Capo had caught King Zoe and Poppa on 8th Street a couple nights before.

They were Black's men from Miami sent to help Chub hold down Delray. King Zoe broke after taking a gruesome pistol whipping from Capo and seeing Poppa's brains blown out by Trap Money. Juvie was still in a shoulder sling, but he was able to torture King Zoe, who had begun to talk when Juvie threatened to brand him.

"So this is King Zoe, huh?" Real inquired, snatching the duct tape from his mouth.

Real then pulled his Glock 9 mm from under his shirt.

"I ain't come to talk and waste my breath. I'ma ask you one time: where the fuck do I find Black?"

King Zoe swallowed hard before he spoke in the best English he could.

"Miami Gardens, 2707 169th. The access code is 1804. I promise you this!" King Zoe truthfully retorted.

Kentucky was noting everything on his iPhone.

"Now, where is Big Chub?" Real asked as he placed the gun to King Zoe's forehead.

"Every Friday he eats lunch at the Haitian restaurant in Delray on 129th. You can't miss it. He eats there with his two lieutenants. He stays in the big blue house on 15th. He plans to kill you at your brother's funeral and kidnap the girl for Black."

"What girl?" Real asked, becoming alarmed.

"Your girl. The girl who Pat used to—!"

Boom! Boom! Boom!

Real pulled the trigger, sending brains and blood everywhere.

"Juvie, clean this up. I gotta get back to Martin. Nobody act on nothing!" Real exclaimed as he punched in Bellda's phone number, only to get no response as he stormed out of the house with Kentucky.

"I can't let them harm Bellda. She's innocent!" Real exclaimed as he jumped in the Durango, accelerated out of the driveway, and called T-Gutta.

"Hello?" T-Gutta answered.

"Brah, get LeLe to get a hold of Bellda for me ASAP!" Real shouted in panic.

T-Gutta was lying in bed, but he became alarmed when he heard the stress in Real's voice. "Yo, LeLe!" he called out.

"Yeah, what's up?" LeLe could be heard in the background.

"Come here!"

"What?" LeLe asked, running into the room.

"Where's Bellda?" T-Gutta asked her.

"She should be getting off work soon, why?" LeLe asked with concern.

"Call her!" T-Gutta told her. He then returned to his conversation with Real. "Brah, what's up?"

"Man, they trying to kidnap Bellda and use her to lure me."

"What the fuck!" T-Gutta exclaimed as he hopped out of bed.

"She's not picking up. She's probably in the building. She told me she's coming over," LeLe announced.

"Fuck!" Real exclaimed.

"Brah, call her job and tell her I said to stay in the building," Real ordered T-Gutta before he hung up the phone. "I can't let them harm her. Too many people have died on my clock," Real explained to Kentucky, who understood exactly how Real was feeling.

"Don't worry, brah. We're five moves ahead of them. Just keep that in mind," Kentucky said.

"The question now is, do I reveal to Polo about Black's location or take this nigga out on my own?" Real asked as they coasted along on I-95 north.

"That's a good question. To have a good face with Polo, you should see what he wants you to do," Kentucky suggested.

* * *

When Bellda stepped outside into the parking lot, she was exhausted from the double shift she had pulled, but she still had it in her to go spend time with Chantele. Bellda looked at her phone while walking to her BMW SUV, and saw a text from LeLe.

She opened it and read: "I don't know what it is. Real wants you!"

Bellda's heart began beating excitedly as she searched her phone contacts for Boo. When she got to his nickname on her phone, she pressed "send" to connect the call, at the exact time her world went black.

The pole that Crazy Zoe used to knock her out did the job well. When she hit the ground, he lifted her over his shoulder and carried her to the backseat of the Suburban that Boxhead was driving. Once Bellda was secured inside, Boxhead and Crazy Zoe took off, leaving her phone and purse behind.

"Damn! You whacked the hell out of her, brah!" Boxhead said.

"Shit! We ain't come to play. I'm glad I only had to hit her ass once. I don't know. I'm thinking about asking Black if I could—!" Crazy Zoe asked.

"Don't even think about it!" Boxhead killed that thought. "I think she's wifey!"

* * *

When Real made it to Bellda's jobsite, her BWM was still there. When he pulled in next to it, he immediately discovered her iPhone and purse on the ground. When he looked at the screen, his heart dropped, and he was hit with a burden of regret. It was a picture of the both of them during the good times. Real then grabbed Bellda's purse.

"Damn it!" Real exclaimed, not believing the reality that she had been abducted by his enemies.

Too much shit going on, man! he thought.

Real quickly hopped back into the driver's seat and sped off on his way to T-Gutta's house. He needed the soldier, who he had built, to come out of hiding. It was now time to put everything on the line for a woman he still loved. Despite his relationship with Mookie and being in denial, Real still loved Bellda.

When Real pulled up to his house, T-Gutta quickly came outside and hopped into the backseat after seeing Kentucky up front.

"They got her, Gutta," Real spoke.

"Big Chub just snatched her from work. I found her purse and her phone, man. But I know where this nigga lives," Real exclaimed as he hopped back onto the I-95 on his way to Delray Beach.

* * *

Boxhead and Crazy Zoe had done well, proving again that Black had surrounded himself with the right men. He was so excited that his prize was on the way that he called for a celebration with Keke and Meme.

As Meme sucked his dick and balls, Black ate Keke's pussy as she straddled his face. Black could never get enough of the twins, and soon he would have three women pleasing him at one time.

"You like my pussy, mon?" Keke purred.

"Black loves yo' pussy, gal," Black retorted in his best English.

"Suck thee gal pussy mon!" Keke purred as Black ate her hairy pussy like a mango.

He loved Keke's bushy pussy. It reminded him so much of the women back home in his country who didn't know what a razor was.

"Ahh, mon! Me coming!" Keke moaned as her body began to convulse while coming to an orgasm. "Yes, mon! Yes!" she cried out in pleasure. She then rotated with her sister.

It was now Meme's time to straddle Black's face. Before she did, she kissed his lips and licked her sister's cum off his face.

"Me want thee mon clean," Meme said as she put her phat hairy pussy in his Black's face as he instantly began eating her out, just like he did to her sister.

* * *

After seeing Director Johnson and explaining that she had the identity of the sniper, Johnson trusted Agent Smalls to bring down Jacob Spears. He was dangerous, and from what Johnny had informed the FBI, he was with an even more powerful man.

Smalls agreed that it was now or never for the takedown. The only thing that deeply bothered her was that Real and Kentucky were somewhere in Palm Beach.

Real pulled a fast one on me. He set up the sniper in position to distract us so both of them could get out of dodge, Smalls realized. *Johnny is now the bait to lure his brother home.*

"He's not picking up!" Johnny said, after persistently trying to locate Real.

"T-Gutta's not at home. The surveillance team says he left in a black Durango. That's Spears's Durango. Put a BOLO on a black Dodge Durango in Palm Beach County," Smalls said over the walkie-talkie to the surveillance agent.

"Johnny, call your mother and tell her to get a hold of Real," Smalls ordered.

"Let's not bring my mom into this."

"Johnny, you have no choice. Remember, you work for us, not us for you. Your brother will be going down soon. If you want to go with him, then push our buttons. Call your mother and get a hold of your brother," Smalls demanded.

They were in Smalls's unmarked car while she talked directly with surveillance teams A and B.

"Alpha DEA. We're now pulling into the Booker Park area of Indiantown. DEA in position."

"Ten-four," Agent Smalls came over her radio to confirm clearance.

As soon as the Smalls ended her conversation with the teams, Johnny did as he was told and called his mom. "Mom, listen. I need you to tell Jermaine to call me. Yeah! No, Mom, I'm okay. Yeah, call me back," Johnny said as he hung up the phone. "She's calling him now," Johnny he said, dropping his head regretfully.

He couldn't believe that he was destroying everything for which his brother had worked so hard.

Lord, he will never forgive me! Johnny thought.

* * *

It was 1:00 a.m. when V-Money had just finished fucking Pimp in the restroom. A couple hustlers were still out moving V-Money's product. Everyone was waiting for morning to see what type of preposterous bond the judge would give Lala and Mookie.

Whatever bond he gives them, it doesn't matter. They are coming home, Pimp thought as she kissed V-Money good night.

"Call me as soon as you get up," V-Money told her.

"Okay."

Before Pimp could finish, the front and back doors to the store opened.

"DEA! Get down now!" the agent ordered V-Money and Pimp.

Without any resistance, both of them complied.

Someone is definitely snitching, V-Money thought as he and Pimp were put into handcuffs.

"She didn't do nothing!" V-Money said as Pimp kept crying.

The DEA had Jake's store roped off. Everyone was laid down and arrested for possession or an outstanding warrant. Johnny had tipped off the DEA, who had brought their K-9 unit inside and immediately found two hundred bricks of cocaine in the walls behind the toilet and in the freezer.

"So, you're the snow man, huh, or Real's lieutenant? We know everything, Varus Hamilton," Det. Harris said to V-Money.

"I don't know what y'all talking about," V-Money exclaimed.

"It ain't me you need to worry about. This case is out of our hands. It's the feds', son," Harris said as he walked over to where Holmes stood talking to Pimp, who was still crying.

"Landa Moor. Fraud is out of our hands too. It seems that your girls, Lala and Mookie, found out earlier than you," Harris explained to her.

"She's in steady denial. Landa, all it took was one bad apple," Holmes added.

"I didn't do nothing like serious!" Pimp cried as Holmes closed the back door to her Yukon.

"Nobody ever does anything," Holmes said.

TWENTY-ONE

Real saw his mother trying to reach him, but he was no fool to give away his location. She had even left him a text: "Johnny is looking for you."

No one other than Real and Kentucky knew that Johnny was an FBI informer.

Real pulled up to a gas station to gas up. He parked and turned off his phone.

"You think they're going to Miami?" T-Gutta asked from the backseat.

"I know they are. They want to deliver their prize to Black, and we gonna be there," Real said.

"I texted LeLe and told her to only text me. She says Jake's store just got raided by the DEA."

"We know," Real and Kentucky said in unison.

"What the fuck y'all know that I don't?" T-Gutta asked curiously.

"Much as I hate to say this, brah, Johnny's been working with the feds."

"What? Chyna Man?" T-Gutta asked, perplexed.

"Yeah, my baby brother agreed to take out the Swamp Mafia," Real explained as he hopped back into the Durango and pulled off.

After speaking with Polo like Kentucky had advised, Real was now acting off of instructions from him. Real hopped back onto I-95 south and gave the highway all he had.

As he coasted, he thought about Bellda. He was remaining calm, but inside he was worried. He missed her a lot, and it had been hell avoiding her when she did her best to come back to him.

She doesn't deserve to die, Lord, Real thought, trusting in his new mentor, Polo, that no harm would come to her while the sun was down. *If he was speaking of some voodoo shit, then I gotta believe him tonight.*

T-Gutta sat in the backseat and was still stunned that Johnny had flipped sides and brought down the realest organization that ever hit the Treasure Coast.

What were his motives and intentions? I can't let these crackas get me, man. We worked hard to get to where we are today, T-Gutta thought as a tear escaped his right eye.

* * *

Bellda was hog-tied and had duct tape over her mouth. She was in the trunk of the Explorer that Boxhead and Crazy Zoe were safely driving along I-95. Black had requested that Big Chub send Crazy Zoe and Boxhead for Bellda, and expected their return the following day.

Bellda was afraid. She had no clue what was going to happen to her. All she *did* know was that the men were Real's enemies. If she was going to die for her man, then she wouldn't beg for mercy. She loved Real unconditionally, even in death.

I love you, Real! Please find a way to know that I'm yours forever. What do you want from me? Are you ready to give me another chance? Bellda thought as tears cascaded down her face. *I love you, Real!*

* * *

Agent Smalls was furious. She couldn't get a location on Real unless he turned on his phone. Being that it was off, no one with even the highest technology could find him.

"You know what, Johnny? Your brother is a smart man. Why would he keep his phone turned off if he didn't know he was being watched?" Smalls asked.

"I can't answer about no one's thoughts or instincts," Johnny said.

"Is that so?" Smalls inquired as she looked back at Johnny, staring him in his eyes. "Are you playing two sides?" she asked.

Johnny laughed, which only made Smalls even more furious.

"Y'all taking the entire empire down. What the fuck do I get out of playing two sides?" Johnny questioned.

"He has a point!" Sullivan spoke up from the passenger seat.

"Whatever!" Smalls said as she started up the Tahoe and put it in gear.

"Where to?" Sullivan asked curiously.

"Martin South Hospital," Smalls said. "I need to see my partner."

She killed the engine when she arrived at the hospital five minutes later.

"I won't be long. Communicate," Smalls said, showing and waving her walkie-talkie at Sullivan.

Agents Smalls exited the Tahoe and walked inside. She showed her badge and quickly got back to Davis. When she entered his room, she was surprised to see that he was up watching television.

"Hey there!" Smalls said shyly.

She hated hospitals since that's where she had last seen her mother on her death bed.

"Rough day, huh?" Davis asked while adjusting his bed to sit up.

"Yeah, a lot of deaths, I'd say, in one day," Smalls retorted.

"How is it going? Let me guess: Sullivan is giving you more than his ass to kiss, huh?" Davis asked.

"How'd you know?"

"Phone, phone, phone," Davis retorted while holding up his cell phone.

"How's the leg?"

"You mean thigh?" Davis corrected. "Nothing major. I was saved on time, or else I would have bled to death."

"Thanks for being there for me. I don't think he wanted us to die, or else he had his chance. Wouldn't you agree?" Smalls inquired.

"It's a game to him now. So, we have to play a little game with him too," Davis explained.

"What's that?"

"Don't follow him until we're ready to bring him down," Davis said.

"At the moment—!"

"He's AWOL with Real. I know this. Don't worry. Real will not miss his brother's funeral," Davis explained.

"So, look for him at the funeral?"

"Most definitely. We'll get Real and then resume seeking Black. Neither of them is dumb enough to be the bait for one another. Johnson wanted Real, and we got him," Davis said.

"That's why I came here—"

"Missing person report on a Bellda Success. That's Real's girlfriend. We have a phone ping in Hollywood!" Sullivan said over the radio to Agent Smalls.

"Hollywood, Florida! Could that be Real?"

"No, that's Real walking into Black's trap. Kidnap Bellda to get Real where he wants him. I saw it a mile away. Follow that ping. He's going wherever Black is going!" Davis shouted to Smalls, who quickly stormed off from the room and made a dash outside to her car.

"To surveillance. Follow that ping. I repeat, we're moving on that ping."

"Man, y'all can let me out right here!" Johnny said.

"Get out!" Smalls and Sullivan both shouted in unison.

Sullivan quickly hopped out and opened Johnny's door to let him out.

"We'll be in contact when this is over," Smalls said.

"Alright, pig!" Johnny said as he strutted off to get away from the FBI agents as quickly as possible.

"We're going wherever that ping stops!" Smalls said over the walkie-talkie.

"Ten-four," her team responded back.

* * *

Coy heard his pit bulls barking persistently, and knew that they only barked when there was prey or something amiss.

Woof! Woof! Woof!

Coy got out of his bed with his wife, Tangy, and grabbed his shotgun in case it was a coon out trying to tear the garbage loose. He walked out back, flicked on his back porch light, and walked toward his barking dogs.

Woof! Woof! Woof!

"What's all that noise?" Coy yelled at the dogs.

"DEA! Drop your weapon now or we will shoot, Coy Dean Bell," Agent Taylor said, ready to pull the trigger.

Coy did as he was told and dropped the shotgun.

"Put your hands-on top of your head and slowly go down to your knees," Taylor instructed as he kept his gun trained on Coy.

Again, Coy followed all orders until they rushed him and slapped cuffs on him.

"So, where do we start, Mr. Trafficker?" Taylor asked as he walked Coy to an unmarked Yukon.

Coy knew the procedure well: don't talk without a lawyer.

So, Coy simply let Taylor bump his gums until he showed up at the Martin County Jail.

"What's my bond?" he asked.

"Like everyone else. You'll see a judge in the morning," Taylor said as he let the Martin County deputies book Coy on twenty-five trafficking charges.

Coy just knew he wasn't going to get a bond and that somebody was talking.

TWENTY-TWO

Juvie and Capo caught on quickly that everyone in the Swamp Mafia was falling. After Coy had been picked up an hour ago, Juvie, Capo, and Trap Money were on I-95 going north until they made it to Georgia, where Juvie and Capo's mother lived in Decatur. They were paranoid and realized that to be free on the streets, they'd have to stick and move.

"Somebody telling?" Trap Money exclaimed while driving the Suburban.

"Man, I've been saying that from when they hit Lunatic. Sad thing about it, a nigga don't know who it is!" Capo said.

Juvie was tired of talking about who could be the rat. It could be anybody, and with no evidence, pointing fingers was just not him. Juvie was glad to be leaving Martin County and Florida. Krystal had promised to move to Georgia the next month and Shaye did too. So neither Juvie nor Capo was losing anything or leaving anything behind but the streets.

On the other hand, Trap Money would have to adapt to the Georgia lifestyle. He was a straight country boy, and where they were going was the city. But Trap Money would easily adapt to the fast life in Atlanta once he saw how Juvie and Capo hugged the block, and he'd have the Georgia peaches going crazy.

It was a blessing for them to leave Florida without anything to think about. They were going to miss their grandmother, Mrs. Anderson, but they would also make brief visits. If the Swamp Mafia was falling, then they would too, if they stayed and got caught. The odd thing that didn't make sense to Juvie and Capo was that of the traps that were kicked in by the DEA, the biggest was Jake's store.

"Where the fuck are Real and T-Gutta?" Capo wanted to know.

"Shit! I bet them niggas doing the same shit we doing!" Juvie retorted.

"I hope so. I know them niggas smart," Trap Money added.

"We cleaned up good. Only thing I hate is that Coy is in jail. The computer says twenty-five damn trafficking charges," Juvie said.

"You think the crackas got pictures of us?" Capo asked.

"They probably do, but do they got us doing shit?" Juvie exclaimed.

"I hope not, brah."

"Shit! We all hope they don't got shit. If they do, they got to come to Georgia, and we know how to make their ass run it. Fuck the law!" Juvie yelled.

* * *

With her red and blue lights twirling, Agent Smalls sped up I-95 doing ninety miles per hour, with more FBI agents following to assist her. After relaying the news to Director Johnson that Bellda Success was Black's actual bait to lure Jermaine "Real" Wilkins into a trap, Johnson had the FBI in Miami on standby following the ping of Bellda's phone.

"Black is a smart and bold man!" Smalls said to Sullivan.

"Well, he's not too smart, or else he would have seen you guys coming alongside him like Real. So I give the credit of intelligence to Real," Sullivan retorted. "They're entering North Dade now," he added.

"North Dade. Black Dodge Durango," Smalls screamed into her radio.

"Ten-four," the agents in Miami responded.

"We're going to take both of them, and then I will get a chance to meet Mr. Spears. It's personal," Smalls said.

After feeling the impact and pain still in her chest, Agent Smalls wanted Kentucky to feel something worse. Davis said if he ever got to Black, he would kill the man dead.

Don't worry, baby. I will make sure he's a dead man once I shoot him between his eyes, she thought.

Davis's vengeance was hers, and she would do everything in her power to lay Black six feet deep, even if it resulted in her losing her life.

* * *

FBI agents Brown and Lucus were set up looking for the black Dodge Durango at the exit of Carol City. They were good friends with Davis and had been on the force with him from the beginning. They also knew how important it was for Davis to catch Black.

"Do you think this is really him?" Lucus asked Brown, who was following the ping from Bellda's phone.

"I think!"

"Shit! My fucking screen froze up on me, man. Come on!" Brown exclaimed, hitting buttons on his laptop to try to unfreeze the screen.

Agent Lucus looked down at the screen and shook his head.

"Fuck!" Brown exclaimed.

After he completely shut the system down, Brown impatiently waited for the laptop to reboot. He never saw the black Durango pass with the blocking semitruck. It was 4:45 a.m., and the traffic was still heavy from people leaving nightclubs as well as going to work.

* * *

Black had four of his men standing outside guarding his palace and awaiting Crazy Zoe and Boxhead's arrival. When they saw the Explorer pull up to the gate, they racked their AK-47s for caution. When they saw the hand reach out to access the code to gain entrance, they relaxed when the gate rolled back. As the Explorer pulled in, the Haitian mafia guards never saw the creeping threat behind the Explorer. It was too late for any of them to react as Snake and Bo-Bo ran back to the gate and waved in Real, who then pulled the Durango in and parked behind the Explorer.

* * *

Crazy Zoe and Boxhead had safely made it to Black's palace. When Crazy Zoe rolled down the window to access the code, Kentucky had both of them in his M-100 scope. He first trained his scope on Boxhead in the passenger seat.

"There we go. Look at the camera," Kentucky said as he pulled the trigger.

Crack!

Boxhead's head exploded in a gruesome splatter of brains and blood onto his window and windshield.

"What the—?"

Crack!

Before Crazy Zoe could fathom, Kentucky pulled the trigger.

T-Gutta ran from across the street hidden behind bushes and made a dash toward the Explorer. He found Bellda in the trunk and quickly grabbed her in his arms. He placed her on the ground, cut the ropes binding her arms and legs with a pair of bolt cutters, and then removed the duct tape covering her mouth.

"Oh my gosh, T-Gutta. Where's Real?"

"He's okay. Let's get you out of here!"

"No! I can't leave without Real!" Bellda exclaimed.

"Bellda's here," T-Gutta said, giving her back her phone, "Real will be close. Let's go!" T-Gutta said as he ran away down the street with Bellda.

Halfway down the road, they met up with a black limousine. T-Gutta hopped inside with Bellda, and Polo sat awaiting them.

* * *

"They're leaving. They stopped briefly at 2707 169th, and now they are heading south," Agent Smalls said into her radio.

"I don't understand how Brown missed them!" Smalls said to Sullivan.

They're going south. What is going on? Smalls thought, perplexed as she continued to follow Bellda's ping.

She sent a small team to the address they had briefly stopped at to make sure Bellda wasn't left behind. Smalls looked at her watch and saw that it was 5:25 a.m.

What a fucking long day! she thought. *I miss you, Tod!*

* * *

Black and the twins were still enjoying themselves. Drinking and fucking were all that the twins wanted to do. The

Haitian music playing from a hidden surround system had the trio in their groove. Black was still waiting for Crazy Zoe and Boxhead to arrive. Black couldn't wait to taste Bellda's phat pussy. Just thinking of her made him erect for the umpteenth time that night. When Meme saw Black's dick standing at attention, she placed her glass down on the edge of the Jacuzzi and climbed in his lap and straddled him.

"Thee mon want more of—"

Psst! Psst!

Before Meme could get the word out, two slugs landed between her eyes, knocking her backward into the water. Keke began screaming after seeing her sister's dead body and the bloody water.

Psst! Psst!

Snake quickly hit her twice in the back of the head and then walked up on an unafraid Black, who hadn't flinched in the slightest after seeing Meme get shot while straddling him. He was never afraid of death.

Black swiftly submerged in the bloody water, grabbing his Uzi at the bottom of the Jacuzzi, and came up with a fusillade that caught Bo-Bo off guard. Unfortunately, Black couldn't escape the young lion, Real, who was nearby and emptied his Glock .40 into Black's torso.

The force slammed Black into a sitting position on the opposite site of the Jacuzzi. He was still breathing even after Real had released his entire clip. Real inserted a fresh clip and was about to shoot into Black's face to finish, until Snake stopped him.

"No! Let me now!" Snake said, retrieving a sword from his hip.

Blood poured from Black's mouth as he looked Real in his eyes with trembling lips.

"It's over nigga! That's for my—oh shit!" Real exclaimed when he saw Snake decapitate Black's head from his shoulders.

Real had never seen anything like it before in his life.

"Damn, man! You good at that shit!" Real said to Snake as he looked down at Black's decapitated head, the eyes of which were still open and trained on him.

Snake walked over to Bo-Bo and knelt down. Bo-Bo was trembling and trying to speak.

"Cold," Bo-Bo managed to squeak out as Snake bowed his head and began speaking in Creole.

Real looked at Black's headless body and the blood-filled Jacuzzi with the naked Jamaican women, and felt the gain of restored power.

If Black could run from the FBI for over ten years, then I could run forever, Real thought.

His thoughts were interrupted when he saw Snake raise his sword and plunge it inside Bo-Bo's throat.

Damn! Real thought as he walked out of the room with Snake on his heels.

* * *

The FBI agents who pulled up to 2702 169th were taken off guard by a sniper in a tree. Agent Brown knew the sniper's favorite holes to hide in and had spotted the shooter and nailed him after rapidly shooting in his vicinity. Kentucky had taken six shots before he fell from the tree, but he was still breathing and holding onto his rifle. Agent Brown saw movement from the corner of his eye and aimed at Real and Snake coming out of the palace.

"Freeze!" Agent Brown screamed. "Drop your weapon or I will shoot!"

His partner, Lucus, was dead, and he was the last man standing out of four agents. He couldn't trust no one's movement, especially after being sniped.

"Drop your weapons now!"

Crack!

Before Brown could finish, Kentucky sniped him, hitting him in his head. Real ran over to Kentucky under the big oak tree and saw that he was hit up badly.

"Damn it, man!" Real exclaimed, seeing that Kentucky was trying to hold on to all he had left in his body.

"Don't worry, brah," Kentucky tried to speak in pain.

"Don't talk. Please, brah!" Real said as he tried to apply pressure to some of Kentucky's wounds, but he couldn't treat them all.

"Shit man! Yo, Snake! Help me, man. He can't die!" Real cried.

Real was losing his best friend who had stuck by him more than a brother, and who had helped build the foundation of the Swamp Mafia while in prison. Now he was dying in front of him, still trying to help Swamp Mafia stand tall even when everything was falling.

"Man, I'm getting cold. This shit feels crazy, brah," Kentucky said.

When Real saw the bloody golds and the blood trickling down Kentucky's mouth, he knew his friend was gone.

"I love you too, brah. Swamp Mafia!" Real cried.

Real then stood up to leave with Snake, who was now the third man in Zo'pound since Bo-Bo was dead.

"Death comes in odds always," Snake said to Real as they left in the Explorer. "Remember."

* * *

When Agent Smalls pulled over the limousine, she and Sullivan approached with their guns drawn while other agents surrounded the car.

"Drop all windows now!" Smalls ordered the chauffeur.

When the windows dropped, Agent Smalls stared Bellda in her eyes. "Bellda Success?"

"Yes ma'am. What is the problem?" Bellda asked nicely and calmly.

"Are you in any form of danger?" Agent Smalls asked while staring at Polo and T-Gutta.

"No, ma'am. Why?"

"Shots fired at 2707 169th!" Smalls heard the agent scream.

"Shit! Dead end!"

"Take her into custody. Sullivan, let's go!" Smalls ordered the other agents as she hurried away.

"We should have gone to 2707 169th," Smalls exclaimed as she sped to her fellow agents' rescue.

When they arrived, she and Sullivan found backup that was closer than they were, and a damn war zone aftermath. When she found Black's decapitated head, she smiled victoriously.

"I can't even be mad at you, Real. You did us all a favor," Smalls said, with her hands on her hips.

* * *

Dominique could tell that something was seriously wrong with Johnny from the moment he called her to come pick him up from Martin County. Seeing him without his own car was a dead giveaway that something was amiss.

They got a room at a Holiday Inn in Port St. Lucie. After a useless round of sex that was faster than Bolt, Dominique impudently asked Johnny what was wrong. For the first time since his infidelity to his brother, he broke down to Dominique about how he had turned rat on his brothers—the ones that put him in the lavish lifestyle that he lived. He wanted to run away and live where no one knew him, but he couldn't run forever or live with the guilty sin he had committed. Despite hating rats and knowing that they got whatever they deserved, Dominique embraced Johnny and let him cry in her arms.

"I know, baby. I'ma clean up," Johnny retorted as he stood up and wiped his face with his T-shirt.

As his shirt raised, Dominique saw his Glock 21 tucked into this pants.

"I'ma clean up. Give me a moment," Johnny said again as he walked into the bathroom, closing and locking the door behind him.

It only took Dominique a moment to fathom. "Johnny! Nooo!'" she screamed as she ran toward the bathroom door.

Boom!

"No, Johnny!" she cried, knowing he was gone.

* * *

At noon, Real was sitting inside his stolen SUV on 129th Street in Delray at the Haitian restaurant. Just like King Zoe had told him, Big Chub had shown by himself to get his grub on. Real watched as he stepped out of his Benz truck and walked inside. Real then watched him take a seat at a back booth. It was time to make his move.

With his hands in his jacket, Real walked into the restaurant and was hit with the redolence of Haitian food. He kept his eyes on Big Chub as he walked to the back. Big Chub's head was down, looking at his phone. Not hearing from Black for a while gave Chub an eerie feeling that something was amiss.

"Big Chub, we finally meet!" Real said to him.

Real startled Big Chub, who had fear written all over his face when he saw his biggest enemy, Real. When he saw the two Glocks in Real's hands, he shit himself.

"One time. I need a name. Who killed my brother?" Real asked.

Big Chub briefly laughed at Real and then looked into his eyes.

"I killed yo' brother, nigga!"

Boom! Boom! Boom! Boom!

Before Big Chub could finish, Real emptied two clips into him, leaving him lifeless. As the restaurant went wild, Real made his escape with no problem. He was determined to kill every man in the Haitian mafia if he had to for his brother Shamoney.

EPILOGUE

Two Weeks Later

Portmore, Jamaica

Two funerals joined together were too much for Michele. She had lost two sons in the blink of an eye. The Reverend Gary Church in Indiantown was overcrowded. The line poured out into the streets, and the FBI was there too, looking for Real, expecting him to show his face. It hurt Real to miss his brothers' funerals, but he had to do the unexpected. When Shamoney's and Johnny's caskets were opened, Real paused the video screen and looked attentively at his brothers. A retrospection of their childhood, when they were curious about street life, flashed before him:

"Man, I'll shoot first and ask questions later," Shamoney said to Real.

"Same to me, nigga!" Johnny said.

"Man, if we have to do that, then, yeah, but there's money to be made. Look at Tony. He's eighteen. When he was fourteen he had a Chevy Caprice on twenty-fours. Shit! I want that!" Real stated.

"Me too! Shit! We got to rob first," Johnny said.

"It don't matter what we got to do!"

"You okay, baby?" Bellda walked into the living room disturbing Real from his retrospective thoughts.

Real wiped his eyes and then squeezed Bellda's hand on his shoulder. Bellda looked at the screen and saw Shamoney's and Johnny's opened caskets.

"They looked nice and will always be remembered," Bellda stated. "I wanted to let you know that T-Gutta and LeLe are on their way over."

"Yeah, I know!" Real retorted.

The End

BOOKS BY GOOD2GO AUTHORS

GOOD 2 GO FILMS PRESENTS

**THE HAND I WAS DEALT- FREE WEB SERIES
NOW AVAILABLE ON YOUTUBE!
YOUTUBE.COM/SILKWHITE212**

SEASON TWO NOW AVAILABLE

To order books, please fill out the order form below:

To order films please go to www.good2gofilms.com

Name:_____

Address:_____

City: _____ State: _____ Zip Code: _____

Phone:_____

Email:_____

Method of Payment: Check   VISA   MASTERCARD

Credit Card#:_____

Name as it appears on card: _____

Signature: _____

Item Name	Price	Qty	Amount
48 Hours to Die – Silk White	$14.99		
A Hustler's Dream - Ernest Morris	$14.99		
A Hustler's Dream 2 - Ernest Morris	$14.99		
Bloody Mayhem Down South	$14.99		
Business Is Business – Silk White	$14.99		
Business Is Business 2 – Silk White	$14.99		
Business Is Business 3 – Silk White	$14.99		
Childhood Sweethearts – Jacob Spears	$14.99		
Childhood Sweethearts 2 – Jacob Spears	$14.99		
Childhood Sweethearts 3 - Jacob Spears	$14.99		
Childhood Sweethearts 4 - Jacob Spears	$14.99		
Flipping Numbers – Ernest Morris	$14.99		
Flipping Numbers 2 – Ernest Morris	$14.99		
He Loves Me, He Loves You Not - Mychea	$14.99		
He Loves Me, He Loves You Not 2 - Mychea	$14.99		
He Loves Me, He Loves You Not 3 - Mychea	$14.99		
He Loves Me, He Loves You Not 4 – Mychea	$14.99		
He Loves Me, He Loves You Not 5 – Mychea	$14.99		
Lord of My Land – Jay Morrison	$14.99		
Lost and Turned Out – Ernest Morris	$14.99		
Married To Da Streets – Silk White	$14.99		
M.E.R.C. - Make Every Rep Count Health and Fitness	$14.99		
My Besties – Asia Hill	$14.99		
My Besties 2 – Asia Hill	$14.99		
My Besties 3 – Asia Hill	$14.99		
My Besties 4 – Asia Hill	$14.99		
My Boyfriend's Wife - Mychea	$14.99		
My Boyfriend's Wife 2 – Mychea	$14.99		
Naughty Housewives – Ernest Morris	$14.99		
Naughty Housewives 2 – Ernest Morris	$14.99		

Naughty Housewives 3 – Ernest Morris	$14.99		
Never Be The Same – Silk White	$14.99		
Stranded – Silk White	$14.99		
Slumped – Jason Brent	$14.99		
Tears of a Hustler - Silk White	$14.99		
Tears of a Hustler 2 - Silk White	$14.99		
Tears of a Hustler 3 - Silk White	$14.99		
Tears of a Hustler 4- Silk White	$14.99		
Tears of a Hustler 5 – Silk White	$14.99		
Tears of a Hustler 6 – Silk White	$14.99		
The Panty Ripper - Reality Way	$14.99		
The Panty Ripper 3 – Reality Way	$14.99		
The Solution – Jay Morrison	$14.99		
The Teflon Queen – Silk White	$14.99		
The Teflon Queen 2 – Silk White	$14.99		
The Teflon Queen 3 – Silk White	$14.99		
The Teflon Queen 4 – Silk White	$14.99		
The Teflon Queen 5 – Silk White	$14.99		
The Teflon Queen 6 - Silk White	$14.99		
The Vacation – Silk White	$14.99		
Tied To A Boss - J.L. Rose	$14.99		
Tied To A Boss 2 - J.L. Rose	$14.99		
Tied To A Boss 3 - J.L. Rose	$14.99		
Time Is Money - Silk White	$14.99		
Two Mask One Heart – Jacob Spears and Trayvon Jackson	$14.99		
Two Mask One Heart 2 – Jacob Spears and Trayvon Jackson	$14.99		
Two Mask One Heart 3 – Jacob Spears and Trayvon Jackson	$14.99		
Young Goonz – Reality Way	$14.99		
Young Legend – J.L. Rose	$14.99		
Subtotal:			
Tax:			
Shipping (Free) U.S. Media Mail:			
Total:			

Make Checks Payable To:
Good2Go Publishing
7311 W Glass Lane,
Laveen, AZ 85339

CPSIA information can be obtained
at www.ICGtesting.com
Printed in the USA
LVOW01s1010120317
526915LV00008B/493/P